THE BEST OF

FRONTIER

TALES

Volume 1

Pen-L

Published by
Pen-L Publishing
PO Box 4455
Fayetteville, AR 72702

© 2012 Pen-L Publishing
All rights reserved
Printed and bound in USA

First Edition

ISBN: 978-0-9851274-0-4

Cover art *Cowboys in the Bad Lands* by Thomas Eakins, 1888

Visit our web site at www.Pen-L.com

Dedicated to everyone who's smelled the campfire smoke and

peered back into time at the vast western frontier of yore.

Table of Contents

THE BEST OF FRONTIER TALES
VOLUME 1

PREFACE

Frontier Tales started out because I was frustrated. I had a Western short story I wanted to publish, but I couldn't find anywhere to submit it. I talked with my friend and mentor, Dusty Richards, about it. He told me how the magazine markets are drying up, how the mainstream publishers were backing away from Westerns, and about the uncertainty that's facing new authors.

I was just a beginner at this fiction writing business. I couldn't do anything to influence the mainstream media or anyone else. But in my nine-to-five world, I'm a computer engineer and websites are one of my specialties. It occurred to me that I could create an online magazine devoted to Western short stories. I couldn't rightly publish my own work there (self-publishing wasn't quite as acceptable then as it is today) but I could provide a venue for other writers. And that's what I've done.

A lot of stories have now seen the light of day and a lot of authors, new ones as well as veterans, have gotten exposure they wouldn't have otherwise. Most importantly, readers have had a chance to see some new tales. They've told me they like them. They've voted on them. Now, here are the best. Enjoy!

~ Duke Pennell, Editor

Dusty Richards –

If there was a Saturday matinee, Dusty was there with Hoppy, Roy and Gene.

He went to roundup at seven years old, sat on a real horse and watched them brand calves on the Peterson Ranch in Othello, Washington. When his family moved to Arizona from the Midwest, at age 13, he knew he'd gone to heaven. A horse of his own, ranches to work on, rodeos to ride in. Dusty's mother worried all his growing up years he'd turn out to be some "old cowboy bum."

He read every western book on the library shelves. He sat on the stoop of Zane Grey's cabin on Mrs. Winter's ranch and looked out over the "Muggie-own Rim" and promised the writer's ghost his book would join Grey's some day on the book rack.

In 1992, his first novel, *Noble's Way*, was published. In 2003, his novel *The Natural* won the Oklahoma Writer's Federation Fiction Book of the Year Award. In 2004, *The Abilene Trail* won the same award. Since then, he's had over 100 novels published, won two Spur Awards from the Western Writers of America, a Wrangler Award from the National Cowboy and Western Heritage Museum, and was named in a True West Magazine poll as the Greatest Living Western Author.

WHEN THE JINGLE BOB JOB WAS OVER

Dusty Richards

Billy Tom Tabor was no chuck-line-riding cowboy. At fifteen, he'd been to Abilene with Herman Brooks' herd. Two more trips up the Chisholm Trail in preceding years made him a veteran of the cattle drives; next he took the job as jingle bob boss on the Half-Circle X outfit. But in a financial hard spot, old man Yarborough blowed his own brains out with a shotgun and the bank dispersed the ranch and cattle.

He'd found day work with a few outfits, but nothing permanent. Short and banty-legged, he did one thing well – cowboy. But when folks learned that he'd once been a boss, they shied away from hiring him for ordinary work. Drifting through the Hill Country, a man told him about the great dance they had every Saturday night at the McFarland Flats School House.

"Where is this place and do they let strangers in?"

"Why lands sake, Billy Tom, you'd fit right in with them folks," his new found friend assured him.

"Reckon if'n you'd make me a map, I'd ride up there and see."

So with a good map in his mind, he took a long bath in a crick, shaved off his whiskers before a cracked mirror hung on a tree. Bought a new shirt and pants at a general store. In his still-starched duds, he rode up there on Saturday.

Arriving in late afternoon he found there was lots going on – women cooking over some hardwood fire pits, kids running about playing and screaming. Men tossing horse shoes. Looked like there soon would be a typical Texas dance and pot luck to him. He hitched his cowpony Buster to a long empty rack and then used his thumb to push his felt hat up some to look over the whole operation.

"Stranger," someone called out and he looked around to see who she meant.

It was a tall willowy-figured woman who was waving for him to come over to her cooking operation. He quickly acknowledged her and hurried over with his hat in his hand. "What can I do to help you, ma'am?"

"I've got all this wood, but it's in too big a hunks to build a hot fire. I'd trade you a couple of dances for some split wood if you've got the time."

"Ma'am, I'd be proud to split you some wood."

"I ain't ma'am. My name's Lorraine. Lorraine Hale."

He made a small bow for her. "My name's Billy Tom Tabor and I'm proud to meet you."

"The pleasure is all mine. The axe is on the wagon, see it?" She pointed to the double-bitted one on the side of her unpainted farm wagon.

"Yes, I do." He strode over, undid it, then run his thumb along the edge. It was mighty dull and the other side the same. "You wouldn't have a file or stone to sharpen it would you?"

"It's in the side box somewhere." She indicated the tool box built on the wagon. When he raised the lid, he realized the man built it was much taller than he was. No way he could stand on the toes of his boots and ever see inside it.

"I'm sorry," she said, stepped over and produced both tools for him.

He thanked her and took them over to a large block. Man, she was tall. He doubted she was hardly impressed by a man who was too short to see in her tool box. He sunk the ax in the block and used the file, then the stone until he was satisfied that edge was sharp then he did the same to the other side of the axe.

The tools set aside, he began splitting out the block, swinging the axe above his head and each time cleaving off a block of wood was about an inch thick. Then splitting it into smaller sticks. He never noticed her coming over until she stood over him.

"Your momma must have taught you how to split wood."

"I've split enough in my day."

"Well, you do a pretty job of it." She bent over and began to gather up an armload.

"Here, I'll do that for you."

Half straightened, she met him face to face and shook her head. "I don't want you to quit busting it."

"No problem, ma'am."

She shook her head again "My name's Lorraine."

"I know and I'm working on that too."

Her laughter sounded free as she went back to her cooking pit with the sticks. He was swinging the axe hard and his results were identical. He was busy using his foot to right a new chunk when a red-headed boy of maybe eight, with his hands drove down in his overall pockets, joined him.

"Howdy, neighbor," Billy Tom said, letting the axe's blow bite deep in the block. It required two more licks to split open the oak.

Then the boy spoke, "I ain't no neighbor. My name's Micah. She's my maw."

"You're mighty fine-looking young man. Mine's Billy Tom."

"That's Mr. Tabor to you, Micah," she called out to her boy.

"Kin you dance?" Micah asked.

"I've danced some, why?"

"Cause mom likes to dance."

"She does?" He spit in both hands and went back to swinging the axe.

"Yeah. She does and she don't get to dance much."

"Why's that?"

"Micah, that man doesn't need you bothering him," she said, busy making sourdough on the wagon tailgate.

"Oh, he's fine, ma' – Lorraine."

"Micah, you just go play with those boys your own age."

Billy Tom drove the bit in a new block and then went to loading up the new supply on his arm to take to her fire. He watched Micah saunter off toward the kids playing games along the crick.

"He wasn't hurting me none."

She never looked at him. "I heard him talking about me. I guess I was rather forward offering you dances for my firewood."

"No, you needed wood and I needed to meet you."

She blushed. "His father was killed at the end of the war in Mississippi. Micah never knew him. He was only two when Matthew died."

"War did some terrible things to folks."

"Half the men folks around here never came home."

"I see why there isn't anyone to dance with up here."

"How old are you?"

"Does it matter?"

She clapped her hands of the flour from kneading the dough. "I'm a lot older than you are."

"I'm twenty-one."

She chewed on her lip. "I guess three years ain't much."

"Naw, I've been on my own since I was fourteen."

"What brought you up here?"

"A man down in Benderville said you all had a fine dance and supper up here every Saturday night."

"We do." She moved to grease her Dutch oven.

"I imagine you do have a swell one. Do you have a place?"

"I do."

"Who chops your wood for you at home?"

She shrugged.

"I'd say you do."

"Most of it. How do you know that?"

He chuckled. "That axe were so dull it must have worn you out to use it."

She laughed and tossed back her light brown hair with the back of her hand. "It was dull alright."

"You have stock? A farm?"

"I try to do that. An old Mexican works for me – Juan. He's a big help and I can hire some cowboys for roundup." She wrinkled her slender nose. "They don't like women in

7

their cow camp. I've been running things for five years – even longer than that since he went off to war."

"A pretty woman like you should have found a man by now."

She looked a little affronted by his words until he realized he'd been talking out loud what he'd been thinking. How could he fix that?

"I didn't mean nothing bad or disrespectable about you –"

"Oh, I've met men I thought I liked. But –"

"You don't have to explain to me, Lorraine. I've met women before and hard as I tried they never worked out."

"Where are you headed?"

"I'm looking for work. Folks hear that I've been a boss once they won't hire me 'cause they figure that doing work would be beneath me."

"Handy as you are at sharpening tools and all, I bet you could find a job around here."

"I'll look for one. And Lorraine, if I'm too short to dance with you, you don't owe me no dances."

"Too short. Why Billy Tom, I'd be proud to dance with you."

That settled, she baked her biscuits in the Dutch oven. Later he helped her haul the food up to the school house. At the plank tables she introduced him to every one of the women. And he could tell they were too polite to question him much, except one sharp eyed hen who asked, "Where are you from Mr. Tabor?"

"Waco."

Acting satisfied, she nodded. "I have kin up there. My uncle Clarence Barr."

"He's a blacksmith or was the last time I was there."

That satisfied her and she went back to straightening out the various dishes. The aroma filled his nose. He'd only eaten a snatch or two of beef jerky that day and his belly walls were rubbing together inside. But it wouldn't be long till they went to serving.

One gal swishing a fly away said, "It'll all be cold and spoil if they don't get in here soon."

The preacher gave a long prayer and the line started. Lorraine pushed him in place. "This is no place to be bashful."

"I'll try not to be."

Why did he feel so comfortable in her presence? He was a head shorter than her but it didn't seem to bother her. Still, he didn't want to get his hopes too high. Micah came in and stood in front of him.

"You wash your hands, young man?" she asked, turning around.

"Of course."

"Good, now mind your manners."

"Yes, mother."

Billy Tom winked at him and the boy grinned like they shared a big secret.

Supper went well. The three of them sat on a bench along the wall and Micah told him who everyone was and where they lived. It was like rain water on a duck's back. He shed lots of it. After all that he could eat and pecan pie on top of that, the musicians started up.

He worried a lot about having two left feet and even gave a small prayer that his boots didn't get tangled up. And when the lead fiddle player struck up the waltz, he rose and bowed to her – then they joined hands and went whirling around the floor like feathers. He felt as tall as he'd ever been in his life and they made great dance partners.

To his shock, no one asked her to dance. So they spent the entire night dancing and sipping lemonade during breaks. When it was over he couldn't believe it had happened nor could he recall anything they'd even talked about.

Going back to her wagon, he led his cowpony Buster up to be hitched with her team. Then she undid his bedroll while he stripped open the girths. "This ain't going to ruin your reputation, me sleeping up here tonight?"

"No, but thanks for thinking of me."

"No problem."

Micah in bed in the wagon, they stood loosely holding each others' hands under the starlight.

"Matthew had big plans for our place. "Course a woman by herself could never do all that."

"The place must have lots of potential."

"It does. I have some good bottom land that grows corn. I can't farm it all and I have lots of pasture under wire and stake fence to keep in my goats and sheep. I run about fifty mother cows on the range land."

"Sure must be lots of work for you."

"It sure beats working for the other fellow."

He shrugged. "If a man could even find work."

"I can tell. You aren't afraid of work."

With a bob of his head, he agreed. "I guess I'm not."

Then he did something he never figured out how he ever did – he reached up and pulled her face down and kissed her.

After they parted, he said, "I ain't much of a man, but I'm wiry."

"Billy Tom Tabor don't you ever say that about yourself again."

"I won't. Cross my heart and swear to die."

Three weeks later they were married at the McFarland Flats Schoolhouse. Over the years, Billy Tom and Lorraine Tabor built a large ranch up there in the hill country. And he always blamed losing his job as jingle bob boss as what brought them together.

Micah, who he adopted and changed his name to Tabor, followed in his boot steps and made the TYT ranch even bigger. There's a large marble marker in the cemetery by the school house. It says *They met at a dance and waltzed all over Texas together.*

The End

Kathleen Sprayberry —

KC Sprayberry loves reading. More than that, she loves writing stories for young adults and middle graders or westerns about a time when things were simpler. Her interest in telling her stories goes back to her high school years, where she excelled in any and all writing classes. While she spends many days researching areas of interest, she also loves photography and often uses it as a way to integrate scenery into her work. Currently, she is hard at work on her first single title release: *Softly Say Goodbye*.

Working also as Kathi Sprayberry, she has many projects with Frontier Tales and another western project: *The Call Chronicles* available on the internet. She lives in northwest Georgia with her husband, youngest son, and an idea-invoking cat, Fireball. Those interested in what's happening next for Kathi Sprayberry may check out her blog http://outofcontrolcharacters.blogspot.com or her website at www.kcsprayberry.com

BROTHERS UNDER THE SKIN

Kathi Sprayberry

On a cool mid-March evening, long after the decent, law-abiding citizens of Tombstone had taken to their beds, Morgan Earp pushed through the batwings of Campbell & Hatch's Saloon. Thumbing back his Stetson, he crossed the expanse of beer stained floorboards to where older brother, Wyatt, and their gambler friend, Doc Holliday, played pool.

"Sorry it took so long," Morgan said. "Lou felt uneasy about my leaving."

"One of these days," Doc drawled.

"Don't finish that thought." Wyatt lobbed a pool cue across the table. "Go ahead and break, Morgan. I don't have much time before I have to make my rounds."

A badge proclaiming Wyatt's position as Tombstone's City Marshal decorated his black coat. The mayor placed it there three months ago, after an ambush nearly killed another of their brothers, Virgil.

"Things heating up again?" Morgan lined up his shot.

"Not really." Wyatt sighed. "Sure wish Behan would settle the cowboys."

"Just an observation," Doc drawled. "Seems like you

and those good old boys are more alike than you realize."

"Right." Morgan laughed.

Comparing the invincible Earps to the cowboy gang was unbelievable. Doc knew better. He and Wyatt were long time friends since the gambler foiled an attempt on Wyatt's life. Folks often said where they found one the other showed up eventually.

"Look at that fool." The shout came from across the street.

Doc sidled across the room and peered through an oiled paper window.

"Trouble's brewing."

"Tell me about it." Wyatt squinted at the windows. "Do you see miners or cowboys?"

"A bunch of miners hasslin' Billy Claiborne." Doc snickered. "Probably giving him a hard time about his unnatural ways. Ain't right, a man wanting to be with another man."

"Bet there's no sign of Behan." Morgan moved for a better angle.

"You nailed it," Doc said.

"We might get home before sunrise." Morgan pulled back the stick.

As he slid it forward, a boom rocked the room. Burning pain lanced his back.

He clutched the table, his fingers digging into the green felt.

Pain spread in all directions and Morgan gasped. Another shot penetrated the fuzziness blanketing him. Doc dove under the table. Wyatt brushed a hand through his hair and turned toward the wall, his features stretching into anger at the sight of the bullet riddled planks.

"Wyatt, get over here." Doc scrambled to his feet.

"Morgan's hurt."

Hands grasped Morgan from behind as Doc lifted his legs. The pain grew to excruciating proportions when they carried him to a sofa in the back room.

"Get a doctor," Wyatt ordered Doc.

After what felt like an eternity, the sawbones rushed in and dug at the injury. Screaming, Morgan clung to Wyatt while begging for release.

The howls rebounded off the walls, reaching into Morgan's soul. This was worse than the injury he suffered during the OK Corral shootout.

A lifetime of agony later, he fell limp. "Guess that's the last game of pool I'll ever play."

What would people think of him, of the undefeatable Earps, after tonight?

Consciousness fled.

Morgan rose from the couch, stretching and feeling his back. Nothing greeted his questing fingers. Puzzled, he moved in the direction of the doorway, where Wyatt conversed with Doc.

"What happened?" Morgan asked.

"Nothing's gone right since October," Doc muttered. "Hell, he was just thirty."

"Should have killed Behan after the shootout." Wyatt snarled at a group of men on the boardwalk. "The cowboys would have moved on with that lousy sheriff out of the way."

"Back to the game, big brother," Morgan said. "I won't let you quit, not when I was winning."

Wyatt remained where he was. Puzzled by his lack of reaction, Morgan touched him. His hand slid through

Wyatt's arm.

"Feels like I'll never get warm again." Wyatt shivered. "I can't believe Morgan's gone."

"Damn!" Doc hacked out a cough and spit onto the floor. "Behan shown up yet to explain why he ain't arrested those damned cowboys?"

"Behan won't show his face tonight." Wyatt clenched his jaw. "I'll kill that bastard sheriff if he gets near me for letting Ike's gang do this to Morgan."

Neither acknowledged Morgan. Puzzled, he touched both. Wyatt and Doc shivered but never looked away from the street.

Morgan rubbed his forehead and reflected on the evening. He, Wyatt, Virgil, and Doc attended a show at Schieffelin Hall. After taking their women home, they gathered at Campbell & Hatch's Saloon for a game of pool. There was a commotion outside the building and then nothing. Absolutely nothing.

"Have Virgil send James or Warren for a couple of wagons." Wyatt said. "You and the others pack clothes for everyone but me. I have to do something." He glanced at the back room. "I'll have our possessions crated and shipped to California."

After following Wyatt's gaze, Morgan nearly came out of his boots. He stood in the saloon but his bloody body lay on the red velvet sofa.

"Say it ain't so," Morgan said. "Hellfire, Wyatt. I'm just thirty."

After Wyatt and Doc walked outside, Morgan floated to the doorway but an invisible barrier held him back. He howled. The sound rebounded against the mountains surrounding the silver mining town.

"Coyotes are mourning him, too," Doc commented. "What are you planning, Wyatt?"

"Nothing less than exterminating the cowboy gang will fill the hole inside me." Wyatt spat onto the boardwalk.

"Remember what you once told me," Morgan said. "Every time you kill a man, even if it's right, that death takes a piece of your soul.

"You'll become what you hate if you go after the cowboys feeling like you do."

Laughter came from a group of men across Fifth. Wyatt shook a fist at them before storming back into Campbell & Hatch's.

"If Behan doesn't get rid of those loafers, I'll shoot them and be done with it." He grabbed a whiskey bottle. "Can't the lot of them have any respect for the dead?"

"Damn it, Wyatt, listen to me." Morgan slammed a fist on the pool table.

Instead of going through the felt-covered wood, a loud thud rocked the room.

Balls scattered across the surface, coming to rest at the bumpers. Wyatt dropped the whiskey bottle. It clattered against the floorboards and a river of alcohol ran under his boots.

"Did someone else shoot at us?" he asked.

"Don't know but I'll get Virgil and the rest going," Doc said.

"We need to move your women somewhere safe."

"Yeah." Wyatt slumped against the bar. "Have the undertaker bring a coffin for Morgan." A dog whimpered under the table. "Get out of here, you lousy cur!"

The batwings squeaked open as Doc left. A woman sidled through the swinging doors, a silk dress revealing her delectable charms. Josie Marcus was a gifted whore, more so than a singer. Until a year ago, she claimed John Behan, Cochise County's sheriff, as her common law husband. Not long after Virgil brought the Earp clan to Tombstone, she succumbed to Morgan's sweet words before turning her attention to Wyatt.

"I just heard." Josie threw her arms around Wyatt's neck. "I'm so sorry."

"Oh, Josie." Wyatt held her tightly. "Those damned cowboys killed Morgan."

"Stay away from her," Morgan warned. "She's nothing more than a lousy whore."

Josie kissed Wyatt, sickening Morgan. He shoved between them.

They shivered before she wandered back into the night.

"Josie, wait!" Wyatt hustled after her. "I'll walk you to the Bird Cage."

Morgan paced around the room, his anger growing with every passing moment. Why was he stuck in this place?

The sun illuminated the mountains before the undertaker came into the saloon. Virgil and Wyatt wrestled a pine box through the door.

"Don't put me in Boot Hill!" Morgan yelled while the undertaker placed his body in the coffin. "Don't make me lie beside the McLaurys and Billy Clanton."

Virgil and Wyatt left with the undertaker's help. They stopped at a wagon parked outside the door and slid the casket into the bed. A loud sobbing from another wagon tore at Morgan's heart. Louisa, his beautiful wife, leaned against

Allie, Virgil's wife, and cried into a handkerchief.

Doc and Warren, Morgan's youngest brother, sat on horses. James, the oldest of the Earp men, controlled the women's wagon.

"Are we ready?" Wyatt asked, taking the reins of the wagon containing Morgan's body.

"Sure are." Virgil, with James' help, climbed onto the seat of the other wagon.

"Let's get out of here. I'm damned tired of this town." Wyatt clucked at the horses and they headed to the west.

"Don't leave Lou alone," Morgan yelled over the swinging doors. "Damn you, Wyatt, don't you dare let my wife be alone!"

A boy appeared the next day with a bucket and brush. He scrubbed at the floorboards until the dried blood became nothing more than a dark stain. After he left, Morgan paced around the room.

There were many entertaining times but Morgan remained at Campbell & Hatch's entry. Not once did he waver in his belief that his family would return. The Earps were strongest together. In all that time, he never saw a sign of his brothers. After many lonely years, the Mountain Maid mine shut down.

Not long after that, the saloons closed their doors. Both Schieffelin Hall and the Bird Cage Theater went dark. Whores drifted away to better pickings in other towns. No longer did miners drag silver from beneath the ground.

Cowboys drove their cattle to Tucson or Dodge City.

When Morgan thought he would go insane from loneliness, tourists arrived to gawk at the spot where he died. To relieve boredom, he threw shot glasses at them or appeared as a misty cloud above the bar.

Most times, people ran away screaming. One afternoon, a boy stared up at him.

"You sure ain't too scary," the kid announced. "It only took one bullet to put you down. Wyatt never got shot, you know."

"So what?"

Morgan did not care if the kid heard him or not. It was excruciatingly dreary living like this. He had always enforced the law, first in Dodge City with Wyatt, and then Deadwood. Both times, they left behind towns where people respected order. In Idaho, Morgan took up the City Marshal position, in charge for the only time in his life. It was also the first time he killed a man. That thought jarred him. He obeyed every known law but some felt he should have held back and waited until the man slept before arresting him.

"Is that why I can't leave this place?" Sighing, Morgan slumped against the pool table. "Get on out of here, kid. Find your parents."

The kid kicked the bar. "Sure ain't what I expected from an Earp. Guess all of them movies lied."

He wandered out the door, the batwings swinging in a lonely wind.

"Life ain't what you expect, kid." Morgan sighed. "Nor death."

January of 1929 came upon Tombstone with an icy blast. Snow coated the streets. On the morning of the thirteenth, a crowd of men hustled through the doors. Frank and Tom McLaury appeared as they had the day they died at the OK Corral with Billy Clanton on their heels. The trio bristled at Morgan but never made a threatening move.

"Why are you here?" Morgan demanded.

"We have our orders," Frank McLaury said. "Can't say anything else until the others get here."

One hour later, Indian Charley Florentino entered looking confused. Curly Bill Brocius sauntered in not long after that, a tequila bottle swinging from one hand. Johnny Ringo appeared near sunset, his red-gold mustache quivering. Ike Clanton slithered through the entryway moments later, his eyes moving from side to side.

Morgan reached for his sidearm. Nothing was there. He checked the holster but it was gone too. Before he reacted, the cowboy gang stood against a wall on the far side of the room, close to where he died.

The doors swung again. James, Virgil, Wyatt, and Warren marched through them.

"Good to see you again," Wyatt said. "We wondered if you'd be with us."

"You're dead?" Morgan had trouble believing that.

None of his brothers looked older than they did the day the Earps and Doc took down the cowboys at the OK Corral. As if Morgan's thought sent a message, Doc stomped into the bar. He grinned, the same one he displayed that fateful day.

"Well, damn! Ain't this a sweet reunion? Break out the cards and whiskey." Doc rubbed his hands together. "I haven't had a decent game of poker since we left this place."

"Better get over here, Doc." Virgil nodded at a hole growing in the center of the floor. "It appears we're about to discover our fate."

Doc joined the Earps. Morgan turned a cold shoulder to the gambler. If not for Doc harassing Ike Clanton, they would have never marched through Tombstone in October of 1881.

"What happened to Louisa?" Morgan asked.

"Not sure." Wyatt shrugged. "I didn't see the family much after your death." He glared at Virgil. "Someone blamed me."

"Tell me my wife had a good life. Tell me she's all right." Morgan grabbed Wyatt's coat.

"None of us know where Louisa is," Virgil said. "She left not long after we buried you. Refused to tell us where she went."

A rumble shook Campbell & Hatch's Saloon. It sounded much like the town had in its heyday, with cattle roaming the streets while cowboys herded them to the broker.

Two men sprang from the hole in the floor. The first was pale green, from his clothes to his skin. He gripped a scythe in one hand. The second had the horns Morgan had long associated with Satan. As they stood between the two groups, a brilliant light pierced the ceiling. A man wearing a pristine white suit with a glow surrounding him floated gently to the floor.

"Why are you here, Gabriel?" the pale green man asked.

"I claim one of these men." Gabriel crooked a finger at the cowboys.

The impossible had happened. An angel wanted an outlaw.

"Johnny Ringo, you devoted your life to protecting those unable to do it themselves," Gabriel said. "Most thought you an unrepentant drinker and gambler but someone noticed your good works. Come with me. There's a place for you."

Johnny joined the being and gazed upward. A massive library appeared in the clouds.

"Now that's what I call a reward." Johnny vanished with the angel. Satan and the pale green man laughed.

"Well, he only took one, Death," Old Scratch said. "That leaves us with the rest."

The Pale Rider had come for him after all these years. Disbelief ran through Morgan. What had he done wrong to invite this afterlife?

"Sure did," Death replied. "Now that we have our booty, shall we get about it?"

"Gabriel forgot one." Satan glanced at Morgan. "I can't take him. Ah hell. I get to pass on the glad tidings again. When will Gabriel stick around long enough to do his own dirty work?"

"What do you mean?" Morgan demanded.

"You'll find out," Death said.

The thundering outside the saloon grew louder. A herd of cattle moved past, fire spewing from their horns and tails. Then a group of horses stopped at the railing, their manes a mass of flames.

"Gentlemen," Satan announced. "Keep the calves with the herd."

The cowboys, Earps, and Doc jerked against invisible strings pulling them toward their fate. Morgan took a step but like the day he died, an invisible wall separated him from his brothers. Without a word, outlaws and lawmen clambered onto the horses and took off after Satan's cattle.

Despite their enmity in life, they worked together to bring the dogies back to the herd. When the excitement faded, Morgan turned to his tormentors.

Before he could demand why they had done this to him, the swinging doors slammed against the walls.

"Why have you disturbed my rest?"

Time had not treated former Cochise County Sheriff John

Behan well. A yellowish cast to his skin announced Bright's Disease, usually brought about by a bullet a surgeon had not been able to remove. Morgan smiled. At least one of his enemies suffered before dying.

Death pointed at the hole in the floor. Four men marched along Fremont, their dusters flapping in a breeze. A gasp blocked Morgan's throat as he gazed at Virgil, Wyatt, Doc, and himself heading for the OK Corral on October 26, 1881.

"John Behan, you incited a battle that brought about more problems than it solved," Satan said. "Your scheme to destroy the Earps and control the cowboy gang failed but you still tried to sow discord. For that, you shall stand between these groups for eternity.

"The hell you say," Behan protested. "I won't do it."

"As if you have a choice," Death commented. "Join the men." With a flick of his hand, he hurled Behan into the hole.

Death and Satan chuckled as Behan struggled to escape his fate.

For hours, the devil and the biblical horseman stared as Virgil shoved the sheriff aside and the Earps continued their march.

"Sure looks like Behan won't ever figure it out," Satan said.

"I'll enjoy tormenting him."

"What about me?" Morgan asked. "What happens to me?"

"Should we tell him, Old Scratch?" Death slung an arm around Satan's neck.

"Always thought he'd figure it out himself," Satan said. "All these years, I thought he was the smartest of the Earp brothers."

"Tell me what?" Morgan demanded. "You have to send me

to my fate. I can't stay here."

"Why should we do that?" Satan asked. "You're not our responsibility."

"You are," Morgan insisted. "Gabriel didn't want me."

"Neither do we." Satan snickered and turned to Death. "Shall I tell him or will you?"

"I've wanted to for a long time but Gabriel wouldn't let us until we gathered all of them in the same place." Death bowed to Morgan.

"You've always been where we wanted you. Give the tourists a good show."

They disappeared into the fiery smoke. Morgan howled and wept.

This truly was hell.

The End

Terry Alexander –

Terry Alexander lives on a small farm near Porum, Oklahoma with his wife, Phyllis. They have three children and nine grandchildren. His work has been published in anthologies by Living Dead Press, Static Movement, Moonstone Books, Paper Cut Publishing, Open Casket Press, Knightwatch Press, Mini Komix, and at FrontierTales.com. He is a member of the Oklahoma Writers Federation, Ozark Writers League, The Arkansas Ridge Writers, and The Fictioneers

DOUBLE EVENT

Terry Alexander

The woman tugged the laces of her best high-topped shoes, tying them in an even bow. "Come on, Ester. Get moving. We need to get there early, give the men a good look at us."

"Do you really think this will work?" Ester tugged the blue dress over her head.

"I've been around a few hangin's and believe me, business always picks up after." She studied her reflection in the small cracked mirror above the night table.

"I've never been to a hanging before, Lola. What's it like?"

"You're not there to watch. You're there to be seen." She smoothed the wrinkles in her dress, a full-skirted yellow outfit worn thin at the sleeves. "They'll remember you later when they get some liquor."

"How do I look?" She pranced from behind the oilcloth partition, her bare feet kicking dust from the floor as she danced circles around the small room.

"Pretty, very pretty." Lola nodded her approval. "Take a couple drops of arsenic with some water. It'll make you look younger. Men like being with a young woman."

"I don't like arsenic." Ester frowned. "It makes me light-headed."

"It'll help bring in the customers."

Ester nodded, her face wrinkled with distaste.

"Be sure you wear those new stockings, and clean up your shoes. You're gonna give these men something to look at." She stroked the younger woman's red hair. "It'll be worth it when we get to a big city. You'll be in big demand. We'll make a wagon load of money."

"Where are we gonna go?" Ester asked.

"Anywhere but here," Lola said. "Someplace where a woman can get an even chance, where we won't be dollar whores."

Ester rolled her eyes; she had heard it all before. Make your money, get out of the business while you're young, find a man and settle down. Deep in her heart she knew Lola was right, but it was hard to see tomorrow from a one room shanty with oilcloth partitions separating the beds.

"Really, where are we going?"

"California; someplace by the ocean, or maybe New Orleans." A red flush crept up Lola's face. "Someplace where we have a chance. You're too pretty to be working these cribs."

"I hope this works." Ester pulled an old brush with several missing bristles through her hair. "I want to leave El Paso, get out and see the world."

"Remember to smile, show your teeth, bat those green eyes, and we'll have them lined up at our door." Lola smiled; the crow's feet stood out prominently around her eyes. "Believe me, when a man's little general stands at attention, they'll follow him into battle and the devil take the consequences."

Ester's hand covered her mouth, stifling her laughter.

28

"Finish dressing, we need to get moving. There's money to be made tonight." Lola winked. "Don't forget to put the extra oil cloths on the beds; I don't want those cowboys ruining my bed covers with their spurs."

"I'll make sure everything's ready." She darted under the rope hanging between the beds. "Who are they hanging?" she asked.

"A couple of Mexicans. They say Pat Garrett brought 'em back from New Mexico and traded them for a fella here they had papers on." Lola dabbed a drop of vanilla extract behind her ears.

"Two hangings at once." Ester fitted the stiff oilcloth over the beds. "I've heard of such things, but I never imagined that I'd ever see it."

"Folks around here are too cheap to spring for two ropes. They're gonna hang two men with the same rope. Ain't any wonder a girl can't make a decent living here. It's bad enough to be a whore, but to starve in the bargain just ain't right."

Ester reached under her mattress and removed a pair of crinkled stockings. "A double event," she said.

"Just like us." Lola gazed at her face in the mirror. "A double event." She looked around the small room. "Get to moving, gal. We want those men to get a good look at us."

The two women strolled down the dirt street, circling several piles of fresh horse droppings. A mixed crowd of spectators gathered, waiting for the spectacle to begin. A jovial mood spread through the mass of humanity. Men hoisted small children to their shoulders, pointing at the cross members. Several walked under the gallows, staring at the underside and the trap door.

A trio of men loitered in an alley off the main street. They passed a bottle between them, trying to go unnoticed. They failed in the attempt. Their eyes locked on the two women.

Lola flashed the three a broad smile. She nodded in their direction. "We'll see them before eight o'clock."

Married men openly appraised the two women, only to receive a swift elbow to the ribs from their mates. Lola smiled broadly, the crowd was growing, this was going to be a good night.

A bustle of activity came from the jail. The hangman exited the sheriff's office, a large black bag in his hand.

"He's gonna fix the rope to the beam." Lola leaned toward Ester, whispering the words softly. "He'll measure out the rope to make sure the drop pops his neck."

"He acts a little nervous. How many hangings has he done?"

"First one he's ever done himself, but he's talked to professional hangmen." Lola said. "They set him straight on the way it should be done."

"They're bringing the first man out." Ester moved through the mob to the front of the scaffold.

"What are you doing?" Lola pushed her way through the tightly packed mass. "Let's move to the back." She grabbed Ester's elbow, pulling her along.

"I want to see it all." Ester shook off the older woman's hand.

Lola shook her head; this wasn't part of her plan. This could ruin everything.

The sheriff walked ahead of the shackled Mexican; two shotgun packing deputies followed closely behind. The big man laughed as he approached the steps.

Lola watched in disbelief. "This ain't a tea party, fella," she whispered.

The planks creaked as the large man bounded up the steps. His continuous laughter filled the air, echoing from the squat buildings.

"Is that man touched?" Ester asked, her voice the faintest of whispers.

Lola nodded. "That's Antonio Flores. Been like that all his life." She held a finger to her lips. "The sheriff's gonna read the death warrant."

A pot-bellied man with a star pinned to his chest brushed a finger across his mustache. He cleared his throat and began his oration of the death sentence. Flores's laughter drowned out his words.

A priest leaned in close to the prisoner's ear. The laughter died in the man's throat at the padre's whispered message.

The executioner fitted the black hood over his head. Positioning the rope properly behind the left ear proved to be a problem for the inexperienced hangman. After several minutes he nodded to the sheriff and padded the short distance to the lever.

Lola held her breath as the lawman returned the nod. The young man pulled the lever. The trap door snapped open and Antonio Flores plunged the short distance to his death.

She closed her eyes. The snap of bone and cartilage silenced the crowd. She glanced at Ester. The younger woman paled, her complexion turned ghostly white. She reached for the girl's hand and gave it a reassuring squeeze.

Two stout men labored with the body, lifting it up to allow the hangman to free the rope from the beam and lower the cadaver to the ground. A grimy-suited doctor stepped under the scaffold. A wreath of cigar smoke circled his head from the stubby butt gripped between his teeth. He rummaged through the bag and removed a wooden tube. He held the cone shaped instrument over Flores's heart, placing his ear over the flat end. He listened for several seconds. "He's gone." he said.

The hangman and sheriff moved to the body. They struggled with the rope, unable to gain any slack in the noose.

"What?" Ester held her stomach. "What are they doing?"

"They're wetting the hemp, trying to get the knot to slip." She shook her head. "They should have bought two ropes."

"Soap, let's try soap," the hangman said. "Lather it in real good, and the rope should slip easily."

"Soap." Lola frowned. "They've already soaped the rope."

A deputy broke away from the mob and ran to the jail. He returned shortly carrying a well-used bar of lye soap. The sheriff and hangman worked the lather into the braided hemp, slowly gaining slack in the rope. An impatient under-taker, his foot tapping the ground, waited to assume control of the body.

"Okay." The young executioner tugged the noose free. "Get the next one ready."

"That's a lot of soap." Lola's hand went to her throat. "They used too much."

Two men wrestled under the dead weight; they carried the body to a waiting wagon, under the watchful eyes of the undertaker.

"This is the one everyone's waiting on," Lola whispered. The sheriff led Geronimo Para from the jail.

"See that fella over there." Lola nodded in the direction of a broad shouldered man with a drooping mustache, sporting a Texas Ranger badge on his chest. "That's John Hughes. Para killed a friend of his some time back. He really wants to see Para hang."

Ester licked her lips. She watched the Mexican walk across the dusty street. The chains on his feet jingled with each step as he slowly ascended the steps.

Para took his place over the trap door. The executioner's hands quivered as he fitted the hood over the burly man's head. Ester moved closer as the lathered rope circled the killer's head and tightened.

"You're getting too close." Lola pulled Ester's sleeve, trying to lead her back into the heart of the crowd. The double clump of the lever and trap door drowned out all other sounds. Time seemed to stand still; Para came to a jarring stop at the end of the rope. The soaped knot slipped from its placement behind the left ear. The lathered braids sliced the tender flesh of Para's throat.

"Oh my God!" Ester screamed. The warm jet of blood from the Mexican's severed jugular covered her face and soaked her dress in crimson. Her hands automatically covered her face, coming away wet and sticky. "Lola, help me," she screamed. "Help me."

Lola's jaw dropped. She stared slack-jawed at the dangling figure of Para, unable to tear her eyes away as the Mexican kicked his life away, a heavy mist of scarlet spraying from his throat. Ester grabbed her elbow, leaving a red smear on the fabric.

"Lola!" Ester shouted. "Let's get out of here. Take me home."

Lola stared dumbfounded at the woman in the red mask. Her mind refused to accept the reality of the situation. The touch of warm sticky hands on her face jolted her numbed mind back to the present.

"Let's get out of here!" Ester shrieked.

The two women ran from the main street, unmindful of the stares and jeers from the crowd. Ester tore at her dress, as they passed through the doorway of the hovel they called home.

"Get these off me." The thin material ripped under her hands. "Get these things off me."

Lola sucked in a deep breath. "Calm down," she said at last, fumbling with the buttons on Ester's dress. "You're not hurt, and we'll have this off you in just a minute."

"Oh God, I'm going to be sick." Ester's hand flew to her mouth. "I'm going to vomit." Her cheeks puffed as the hot bile rushed up her throat.

"Not in here! Get outside! Not in here." Lola grabbed her hand, guiding Ester toward the back door. They made it to the window. Ester stuck her head through the opening and wretched. Her body wracked with spasms as she purged her stomach.

Lola dabbed at her face with a wet cloth. "You'll be all right," she said. "Just calm down. You'll be all right."

"The blood, did you see it? Did you see how it sprayed? I was eight feet away, and it soaked me." Ester wiped the clear sheen of stomach acid from her mouth, removing a small portion of blood. "I can smell his blood on me. I smell like a slaughter house."

"Get out of that dress." Lola pressed the cloth in her hand. "Take this and clean up, as best you can. I'll get some more water." She crossed the room quickly, disappeared out the back door. She returned with a small bucket filled to the brim, her movements splashing water to the floor.

"Oh my head." Ester pressed the heel of her hand to her forehead. "I'm gonna be sick again." A stream of hot liquid struck the windowsill.

"Lord, girl, get yourself together." Lola patted the young woman's back. "We'll have customers here in a couple of hours."

"I can't do it!" Ester stammered, unable to control the trembling in her body. "I can't do it. We'll have to make the money another way."

"Are you insane? This is our big chance. They'll never be another opportunity like this. If we're ever gonna leave El Paso, we have to make a big score now."

Lola stared down at the young woman. Ester returned her look through pained sorrowful eyes. Her face covered by drying blood and fresh stomach slime. "I can't go tonight," she said.

"Think about this, whores are used up before they're forty. They're gray haired, toothless wretches, putting out for a quarter or a dime. This crib is bad but imagine living and doing business in an alley, no roof over your head and no food. If you're lucky, you won't starve or freeze in the winter. Is that the life you want?"

Ester closed her eyes. Tears streamed around the lids, threading down her face. Her shoulders quivered in time to her muffled sobs.

"Make up your mind. We have a great chance to make money and move on to something better, but we have to make the money tonight. It's up to you."

Ester fought back her tears. Her grim face turned to Lola. "Damn you! Let's get the money."

The first men arrived at twilight, a pair of cowhands who stank of sweat, manure and cheap liquor. Lola studied them through a slit in the flour sack curtain.

"Come on, girls." The larger one pounded on the door. "Open up, it's time for company."

The shorter man, sporting a new vest, kicked at the door-frame. "Don't keep us waiting all night."

Lola stuck her head out the door, giving the two a quick glimpse of her tattered underwear. It paid off to give the customers a little glance at the merchandise before the bargaining began. "What can I do for you men?" she asked, her voice syrupy sweet.

"How much?" The short man clad in the new vest asked.

"Right to the point, huh." Lola smiled. "I like that." Her hand rubbed along her chin. "Five dollars each."

"That's a little steep ain't it? Last week it was only two." The short frowned.

The burly man pulled new vest away from the door. He whispered something that Lola couldn't catch. The shorter man kept shaking his head in contrast to the bigger man's nods.

"Are you boys gonna make up your mind or what?" Lola leaned on the doorframe, letting the door swing open, giving the men a good look at her in the fading light. "I can't stand out here all night in my shift."

"We'll go four dollars," the short man said. "But only if we can see the dress."

Lola shook her head. "You can see the dress, but it's five dollars."

"Damn." New vest pursed his lips, the tip of his tongue barely visible. "It's a deal." He hurried through the door, tugging at his waistband. "Where's the other one? I want her."

"Ester, we've got gentleman callers." Lola guided new vest around the partition.

"Send him in. I just love to see visitors." Ester answered weakly. "How are you doing, cowboy?" she asked as he circled the oilcloth barrier.

"Come on, let's finish this up," he said, dropping his pants below the knees. "I wanna see that dress."

Dawn streaked the eastern sky, the new sun driving the darkness and gloom away. The endless line of customers had died away only minutes before. The two women sat at the tiny kitchen table and stared at each other through red bleary eyes.

"Place stinks," Lola said. "Smells worse than a stable."

"Most of those cowboys didn't clean up before they came to town." Ester tugged a blanket snugly around her shoulders. "I didn't think I was gonna make it a few times last night. Good thing you had that laudanum or I wouldn't have made daylight."

"We got through it with you doing the lion's share of the work," Lola said. "I'd love to take a long hot bath and sleep for a week."

"I'm glad it's over with." Ester stifled a yawn. "How much money did we make?"

"Just over a hundred dollars."

"A hundred dollars," Ester repeated. "Enough for the trip to California?"

"More than enough." Lola laughed. "That short fella with the fancy vest made three trips through here last night."

"He showed more interest in the dress," Ester said. "How

did you come up with that idea anyway?"

"The short guy brought it up. He gave extra money for a look at it. I'm surprised so many of them wanted to look it over."

"I'm getting rid of that nasty thing. I think I'll burn it."

"You can sell it if you're of a mind." A smile touched Lola's lined face. "Bart Cantrell treated himself early this morning. He offered fifty dollars for that dress."

Ester's eyebrows pinched together. "Fifty dollars," she stammered. "Why?"

"He claims we stole most of his business last night. The men spent of their money here instead of his saloon."

"That's a lot of money for that dress."

"Believe me, Bart wouldn't make the offer if he didn't believe he could make a profit." Lola scratched at her toes.

"Do we need the money?"

"No, we're pretty flush right now." Lola nodded.

"I know we used this dress last night to make money, but it was a spur of the moment thing." She chewed at her lower lip. "But if we keep it, use it to draw in customers, or sell it for a profit . . . " She stopped for a moment; wrinkles furrowed her forehead, she stared at the blood-stained garment. "If we keep using it, we won't break with our past; we'll always be dollar whores."

"It's your decision. Whatever you want," Lola agreed.

Ester rose to her feet, she crossed the room removing the stained dress from the nail above her bed. "Let's get this over with." Her hand closed on a box of matches. "We need to pack and get started for California."

The End

Greg Camp –

Greg Camp was born in the hills of North Carolina about a hundred thirty years later than was good for him. He has wandered around the southern United States ever since, picking up bits of experience and polishing his curmudgeonly persona. He listens to the Muses whenever they sing to him. Following a star brought him and his three cats to northwest Arkansas, where he is currently trying to repair his sextant.

WINDWARD ROCK

Greg Camp

Dowland sat fingering the butts of his Navy revolvers, wondering how much longer he would have to wait. He was sitting on a shelf of rock a man's height down from the top of the mesa, looking out at the rolling hills and sloping plateau a hundred feet below. The shelf jutted out into the air from the nearly vertical western wall.

Below, the sheriff's men worked their way toward him. They were well out of rifle shot – two miles, at least – but still crouched low and darted from juniper tree to rock to new juniper tree. Did they think that this cover kept him from seeing them, or were they always cowards under the light of the sun?

That sun was three hours from setting. The sheriff and his twenty sucklings would surround the mesa soon enough and sit out of range until dark. Only then would they attack, and Dowland knew that whether or not Morrison showed up, it was going to be a long night.

He stood and stretched, thinking about calling out a greeting when Sheriff Carver got within earshot, but figured that neighborliness had no part to play here. He had seen to it

41

that the sheriff knew where to find him, and he was in no mood for any more gifts. He might have offered the sheriff a horse, like the Saracen knight that he had read about in his history lessons, but someone had already killed his, and that score would be settled tonight along with the total bill.

He climbed from the shelf to the top of the mesa. Had he had his choice of where to fight it out with the sheriff and his men, this mesa would not have been it. There were three easy ways to the top and not much cover, but Dowland smiled, remembering the wisdom that his father had shared with him eighteen years ago that if we could choose the time and place of all of our battles, we would never get around to fighting them.

Of course, his father had said this on the day that the younger Dowland had passed the bar examination, but there were many kinds of battles, and this coming fight was of his choosing. He had led the sheriff out here, rather than letting him be distracted by the possibility of doing greater mischief elsewhere. There were times when a man had to be ready to take a bullet or to give one. Dowland had survived four years of that kind of time, and after coming west, he knew that he would see such times again.

He had had no immediate thought that this was one of them when he was passing through Santa Fe on his way to somewhere else. He just happened upon his friend, Billy Morrison, one evening outside of town.

As he did every day, he had gone out of immediate civilization for a session with Alpha and Omega. That late afternoon, he had set up a coffee tin on the branch of a juniper tree and a spent whiskey bottle on another, both thirty paces away. His first shot at the can had tipped it on its side. The next three, fired in rapid succession, knocked it about on its way to the ground. The last shot flung the battered metal back into the air.

He had Alpha broken down before the can landed. Resting the pieces on a rock, he scrubbed them out and wiped them clean, then reassembled the pistol and loaded five chambers one by one, pouring in a measure of powder, pressing down a wad, and ramming home a ball. He smeared lard across the front of the chambers and capped each nipple. His hands had worked this process so many times that he could do it without looking. His gaze darted about the terrain.

With Alpha cleaned and reloaded, he was about to smash the bottle with Omega when he caught sight of someone approaching. In the dimming light, Dowland did not recognize the man. He grabbed Alpha and brought both revolvers to bear on the man, thumbing back the hammers as the barrels rose.

"Stranger," he said, "I'm just out for practice, but if you're looking to join me, I can accommodate you."

The man's open hands lifted slowly into the air beside him. "Your eyes need the practice if you don't know me."

"Morrison, is that you?"

"The Morrison who was with you when Old Jubilee took us around Washington in Sixty-four? The Morrison who shot off that Yankee's bayonet so as to keep your shirt from having an extra hole in it? I've heard that he might be in these parts."

Dowland lowered the hammers and shoved his guns into his belt and ran over to take Morrison's hand. "So you're still with us in this world of sin."

"Where else would I be?" Morrison asked. The two of

them walked over to sit on a large rock. "Actually, it was about sin that I needed to talk to you."

"Don't tell me that you've found religion. Remember when you brought me back to health after I got shot at Sharpsburg? If I didn't repent my ways when it looked as though that Yankee lead was going to send me to my maker, why would I do it now?"

"It's not the repentance that I want to talk about," Morrison said. "It's more on the subject of punishment."

"What have you done?" Dowland asked, not that the answer would make a difference, but just for general calculation. They had known each other for sixteen years now, meeting as new recruits to the Army of the Potomac. They became the Army of Northern Virginia, having already become friends, and fought against McClellan and Pope and Meade and Grant, occasionally each other, and always the rains, the marching, the wounds, and the increasingly poor food and drink.

Regarding that last enemy, Morrison had proved himself adept at appropriating better supplies without too much concern as to their origin. Bacon, eggs, cheese, and beans were all good in their way, but the one essential was coffee, and that became increasingly hard to get as the war dragged on. The chicory that they often used as a substitute was hardly better than plain hot water. Morrison, though, could feel the presence of coffee beans from miles away. They had saved each other's lives time and again, but that hardly counted in comparison.

Dowland had been thinking that Morrison's current trouble stemmed from some new expression of his friend's old talent, but he realized that things were much worse than just some angry householder chasing him with an aging squirrel rifle. Morrison had the sheriff and his men hot for finding him.

There was no choice: Dowland had to help. Sheriffs were little better than the carpetbaggers who had ruined his home after the War. He hated to see any man put himself above another, whatever the reason. A sheriff's badge made him hungry for vengeance, and seeing that his friend had run afoul of one was just pouring gravy on a good steak.

"Will you help me?" Morrison asked finally.

"Help you? I'd kill him myself if I didn't think that it would rob you of the satisfaction."

"I'll need a horse for now."

"It just so happens that I have one," Dowland said.

"After that, keep your eyes open. Carver has men all over these days."

"My eyes can tell a skunk from a rat, even in this light," Dowland said. The sun had set, and the stars were beginning to shine. The moon would be up shortly. "You wait here, and I'll go get my horse."

It took him an hour to walk into town and bring his horse back. On his return, he offered Morrison a rifle and one of his revolvers, neither of which Morrison needed, and good luck. He watched his friend ride away into the darkness.

On his walk back into town, he passed by the saloons and brothels, figuring that there would be no useful information to be had there until morning. He found the county jail at the end of a line of saloons. The land agent's office sat on the opposite side of the street. A person could get drunk, fined, and propertied all in the space of a few steps, three conditions that he considered to be much the same.

He settled between a saloon and the land agent's office. Pulling a bottle of whiskey out of his bag, he poured it over himself and let the bottle roll a few feet away to come to a rest against a rock. He then lay back with his head on his bag and his rifle and revolvers concealed under his blanket and went to sleep.

The sound of shouting and heavy feet woke him. The sun was just coming up, casting its rays between the buildings. He opened his eyes slightly to see a crowd gathering around what he concluded was the sheriff and his men. They were shoving Morrison, who was tied and hooded, into the jail.

Dowland remained still. The crowd waited outside, looking for more excitement, but when nothing appeared to happen, everyone drifted away, heading off to get an early start on the day's duties in the nearby buildings. Once the crowd was gone, the sheriff and his men came out.

Carver glanced around for a moment with a guilty look. "We've got him, but there's the one more that we need, and then we'll be done with the lot of them. I want them hanged and cold by tomorrow night. Roberts and Mitchell, you stay here, and keep watch over the one we have. Patterson and Oakes, you two go south, and have a look around. If you find anything, one of you come find us. The rest come with me."

Roberts and Mitchell went back inside the jail, and the others left. Sheriff Carver looked around again, briefly contemplating the sleeping drunk that he apparently took Dowland to be, before following his men northward up the street.

Dowland stood and stretched. He gathered up and repacked his belongings. He wanted to charge straight in and rescue Morrison, but he held himself back. The sheriff was not that far gone, and the two guards would still be alert. Better to wait a few hours to give Roberts and Mitchell time to get tired of watching for trouble, tired of arguing over cards, tired of spending the day sober and relatively unemployed.

He hid his rifle in some weeds and then, after turning to the left down the street and walking a few paces, entered the saloon that sat on the side opposite the jail. He took a seat with his back against the wall and his eyes on the jail, which he could see through the window. A girl came up to pour him some coffee and take his order. He supposed that she might have been getting herself born while he was fighting Meade's Yankees at Gettysburg fourteen years ago, but he was probably being more generous with years than was warranted.

By the time his bacon, eggs, and cornbread had arrived, he had drunk his first cup of coffee. A couple passed the window during that time, but otherwise the street had been empty. The two appeared to be from back east, the type that come out to the desert to find what they thought could not be had back home. Dowland felt smug about this, until he realized that he had done the same thing. He had left a lot unfinished in the War, most of it inside himself.

He ate his food and drank more coffee. To give himself an excuse for taking his time, although hardly anyone else was in the saloon at that hour of the morning, he ordered a piece of pie and flirted with the girl, while stealing glances through the windows at Roberts and Mitchell as they busied themselves with the list of things that he had assigned to them earlier.

The jailers' whiskey bottle came out some three hours

after Dowland had taken his seat in the saloon. The two had drunk a glass each and filled another before he stood slowly and walked over to the bartender to settle his bill. On his way out, he dropped a dollar into the girl's pocket as he kissed her on her cheek, making sure that no one saw him do the former.

He strode across the street and opened the door to the jail. Roberts and Mitchell glared at him, looking angry that he was interrupting their day. He pulled the door shut with a bang.

The one he took to be Roberts stood and pulled out his revolver, one of Mr. Colt's new Peacemakers. He was a squat, heavyset man with a face that seemed to have collected some beard in a passing wind. "What's your business here?" he demanded.

"I heard that you'd caught this Morrison here," Dowland answered, waving his hand toward his friend in the cell across the room, "and so I wanted to add some of my own grievance to his score."

Mitchell arose and came over to stand next to Roberts. He had not drawn his own revolver, but he kept his hand on the butt.

"Before we get into that," Roberts said, "you'll need to hand over those guns of yours. We don't want you getting any ideas." Dowland lifted his Navys up from his belt with two fingers a piece, then worked his index fingers into the trigger guards, and pulled the guns out. They hung loosely in front of him. Roberts put his own gun back into its holster and reached out his hands. "I think you'll be pleased to know that this one's going to be hanged just as soon as the sheriff returns."

48

"Ah," Dowland said, "it turns out that I have other plans." In a smooth motion, he flipped his guns over, cocked the hammers, and fired. Roberts and Mitchell both fell to the floor as the merging clouds of smoke drifted over them. Dowland's ears rang as he relieved the bodies of their guns and picked up the keys that were lying next to the two glasses on a desk against the wall. He tossed the keys to Morrison and continued gathering up whatever looked useful.

Morrison released himself and collected the one rifle in the rack and the boxes of rifle and revolver cartridges sitting on a shelf underneath. Dowland pulled open drawers, but Carver and his men apparently had taken most everything of use, and he and Morrison needed to leave sooner than would allow for a ransacking. Roberts and Mitchell had not been dead a minute, and already Dowland could see blinds being drawn and doors being opened.

He and Morrison stepped casually outside. Dowland could feel himself being watched. He walked across the street to collect his own rifle, then the two of them went around the side of the jail to make their escape.

"I heard the sheriff say that he was taking most of his men north."

"That's because I live up that way," Morrison said. "Too bad for him, I already got there before he found me. Thanks for the loan of your horse, by the way. One of Carver's men shot him out from under me, if you're wondering what happened."

"This sheriff likes running up a big tab, I see," Dowland said.

"That's right, and this time, I'd like to see that he pays it."

They made their way on foot into the tablelands to the west of town. Dowland thought about stealing horses, but it was against his nature, and the local populace was now too watchful for that anyway. The land grew ever rougher, which pleased him, since it discouraged the idle townsfolk from following them any farther. There was no doubt, though, that word would get to the sheriff as to where they had gone, and Carver and his men did have horses.

"We'll be in for a hard time of it tomorrow or the day after," Dowland said. He leaned back against the rock under the overhang that they had found. It was the middle of the day, and they were taking a break from the sun. Out in the light in front of them, the rocks of the dry creek bed glinted.

"That we'll be," Morrison agreed. "Most people in town can't stand Carver, but some of them are beholden to him."

"What about your boy?" Dowland asked. "Would anyone turn him in?"

"I've been worrying about that myself. He'll be safe where I left him for a while, but I'd feel better if I could move him. I know a family to the south that are decent folks, but the sheriff doesn't know that I know them. They'd take care of Henry for me."

"My namesake," Dowland said softly. He picked up his canteen and tossed Morrison another strip of jerky to fill the moment.

"I couldn't think of a better," Morrison said. He bit off a piece of jerky and chewed it. "You still haven't asked me what she was doing with the sheriff and his men."

"I figured that you'd tell me as much as I needed to know. Not that it would change anything, since I can't think of an honorable reason to kill a man's wife."

"It's worse than that. They kidnapped her, trying to get me to sell my land cheap to the sheriff. It seems that Carver wants to make himself a little kingdom out here, but my ranch stands in his way. His men took Susan while young Henry and I were digging a new well. When we got back to the house, I found a letter from the sheriff nailed to the door, telling me that I had a day to sell out."

Morrison picked up a stone and threw it. It skipped across the rocks in the creek bed and came to a rest in the dust on the far side.

"I have to thank you for killing Roberts and Mitchell for me. They're the reason that Susan is dead. It seems that they . . . they . . ."

"You don't have to say it," Dowland said.

"Well, Carver figured that he had to kill her afterwards. He had planned on letting her go before his men violated her, but after that, he figured that I'd be too angry ever to let the matter rest and he'd have to kill all of us. I had to listen to him talk out his thinking while he and his men were dragging me to the jail."

"I wish now that I'd have taken longer in killing those two."

"They were fools," Morrison said. He spat out a thoroughly-chewed piece of gristle. "It's Carver who's at the center of it all."

"And his name gives me ideas. I can think of hours of work to do on him."

Morrison looked back darkly for a moment before packing his things. They followed the creek bed until it led them down a cut in a low cliff and out onto a flat expanse.

Dowland saw a mesa in the distance that looked promising. The hard ground beneath his feet seemed even more so.

"The sheriff and his gang will be coming from the north, right?" he asked. Morrison nodded. "Then let's use this land to our advantage. We're not leaving much of a trail here. If you turn back now and head off to get your boy, no one would be the wiser from this ground. I'll carry on and make some signs of my passing, enough for two men. Then I'll occupy that mesa over yonder and wait for you – and for the sheriff."

"He'll find you sometime tomorrow night, I reckon," Morrison said.

The two of them shook hands, and Morrison headed back the way that they had come. Dowland was alone once more. That evening, he made a fire, having come back among the juniper trees. He crossed a shallow creek, and as the water was running rapidly over the rocks, he filled his canteen.

His fire burned steadily on the other side of the creek. He sat with his back against a rock and his several guns at his side, glancing at the flames, but mostly at the land to the north. He dozed for a few hours, waking often, though. Something felt wrong.

Just after midnight, Dowland awoke to the sound of horses coming from the south. He was already concealed by the junipers and only shifted a bit to have a clear view of the glowing embers.

Two men rode toward the dying light, making a show of scanning the ground. Making a show was all that they were doing, since they had been loud enough in their approach to give the deafest of armies alarm and time to disperse. With his right hand, he held up the Peacemaker that he had taken from the jail, wanting to test its qualities on the two whom he figured to be Patterson and Oakes. Omega rested in his left hand, waiting to argue against innovation. One of the men spoke, though, and Dowland held himself from firing.

"It's just as Tarpley said," the man insisted, pointing at the fire. "I see the marks of two men here, and they look to be going west. We've got to ride on to find the sheriff and tell him."

Dowland covered the two with Omega and the Peacemaker as they crossed the creek and rode closer. His trigger fingers twitched, but the rest of him was still. He held his breath as the horses passed by only ten feet away. He waited until the two men rode out of range, then lowered the hammers reluctantly. He had to let them go, so they would report to Carver. Dowland had to work things for Morrison's benefit, no matter how inviting other actions might be.

Lying back against the rock, he concluded that nothing else would need his attention that night and went to sleep.

He awoke with the sun, ate a piece of jerky, and drank some water. There would be a chance for a good meal on top of the mesa, a meal of coffee and bacon and cheese to lure even the stupidest of sheriffs. He worried for a moment that he was laying too much of a trail and would make Carver and his men suspicious, but the performance of the two last night did not speak well for their powers of observation, leaving him to wonder if he ought to paint a sign.

He reached the mesa by mid-morning. The top was a long oval with a dome of bare rock on the far end. Plenty of juniper trees were growing, or trying to grow and failing in the drought, so making a fire would not be a problem. The trees were dry enough, in fact, that he would have to be careful not to set the woods alight.

Dowland built his fire at the top. It was the safest spot to have one, and it made certain that Carver and his men would see it. After only an hour, he saw them approaching from the northeast. At first, they were just a knife's edge that cut open the ground and released an exhalation of dust, but as the day wore on, he could make out the shapes of horses and men. They were riding hard and would be tired when they arrived, yet twenty-one men did not have to be the most alert against one man.

On the western edge of the mesa, beneath the steepest part of the dome, he found a shelf of rock that jutted out from the vertical wall. He wanted Carver to come to the land that spread out below this pulpit. The eastern side sloped down at a shallow angle toward the flat land, and from that side, as well as from the north and the south, the climb to the top gave no pains worth mentioning. He had to draw the sheriff and his men around to the western side, at least for the beginning of the fight. What would happen through the night was too far into the future to plan.

"Sheriff Carver," Dowland called out. Carver and his men had gathered on the flat land beneath the western side, just as he had invited them to do with his fire and his visible movements. "You have arrived at Windward Rock. I've claimed it in the name of Marcus Brutus, Roland, General Lee, and all other good men. I'd welcome you to it, but I have my doubts as to whether you belong here."

"Windward Rock, you've named it?" Carver shouted. He stood some one hundred yards from the base of the mesa, just outside the practical range of the Winchester that Dowland held loose in his hands. Their voices carried easily across the hard ground.

"That's right, and I'd hate to be the man who's standing

downwind of it."

"You studying on breaking wind at us?" a man, either Patterson or Oakes, taunted. Dowland swept his rifle up to his shoulder and took aim, and the man dived for the cover behind a large rock.

"Get up, Oakes, you fool," Carver growled. "He can't hit you from there."

"So that's Oakes, is it." Dowland concluded. "So the one next to him with the moustache trying to hide an idiotic face must be Patterson. They would be the two that you sent south the other day."

Carver turned toward the two and said something.

"While you're lecturing them, put in a bit about how to approach a fire in the dead of night. If they had come any closer to me, I could've swatted their horses on the rumps."

The sheriff whipped around to look up at the dome, then turned, and stomped over to Patterson.

"Oh, go easy on him. He'd be dead right now if I hadn't needed him to do a job for me." Carver landed a punch on Patterson's chin, sending the man sprawling.

"I hope he pays you men well," Dowland called out to the group. "I'm not sure that this kind of work is rewarding enough on its own."

Carver came closer to the mesa. Dowland held his rifle against his shoulder as the sheriff approached. He did not have enough cartridges to waste on hopeful shots, but with each step, the sheriff became more tempting. He stopped when he was about a seventy yards from the wall, close enough to be a disappointment.

"Listen, stranger," the sheriff said, apparently trying a new approach, "I don't know you, and I haven't got anything particular against you."

"You're forgetting about Roberts and Mitchell, then?"

"That's easily done, considering," Carver answered. Dowland knew too well what he was thinking on that score. "They're already forgotten. But as for you, on the other hand, there's no need for any unpleasantness between us. Come on down from there, and let's talk this out like men."

"Better men than you have called me a fool, and only one of them is still wandering this earth."

"And who would that be?"

"Someone of your acquaintance," Dowland answered, "a man named Morrison. It turned out that when he said that to me, he was right. But you, Sheriff, are a poor judge of character if you rank me with the likes of your men." He itched to take a shot. Surely just one would not be too much of a loss. He swung the rifle down, lining it up with Carver. The sheriff turned tail and ran. "I haven't seen such fancy running since my last meeting with a Yankee," he called out. "You ought to hire yourself out for tutoring fawns."

Carver stopped short and spun around. Fanning the hammer of his Peacemaker, he fired off five shots toward the mesa.

Dowland stood still. He watched the barrel of the revolver dancing about. He had never understood the point of emptying one's gun just to make a lot of noise. "Shall I toss you one of the boxes of cartridges that I borrowed from your jail? Keep up like that, and you'll need them."

The sheriff stomped back toward his men and fiddled with the Peacemaker, reloading it. The sun was just setting, and several of Carver's men were lighting a fire, at least they were until he ran over and kicked out the flames. That made no sense, as it had already been established that they were out of range, but perhaps he was still smarting from Dowland's taunt at Patterson and Oakes earlier.

His own fire was dying, and he let it go. He needed his eyes to adjust to the darkness. The evening sky was clear, and a full moon was rising above the horizon.

The sheriff and his men held a council of war. Dowland was glad that he could not hear what they were saying, figuring that he had no need to listen to idiocy. How long it would take them to realize that the mesa could only be climbed on the eastern half?

The wind blew steadily from that direction along the mesa's length. From his position on the dome, he had a clear shot at the flanks, but the slope was obscured by the junipers. If they did come from that direction, he would see the trees shake as they passed and hear their feet crack the dry limbs lying on the ground.

Two hours after sunset, Carver and his men finally began to move. Half of them went around the northern side, while the other half went southward. They kept themselves out of range, though. Their horses were hobbled and left to themselves.

Dowland glared at the rifle cartridges in the cardboard box, wishing that they had multiplied like loaves and fishes while he was not looking, but miracles were something more often read about than received. The rifle held fifteen, and in the box, moonlight glinted off twenty brass disks.

He had loaded his Navys and the Peacemaker with six shots apiece, deciding that eighteen was better than fifteen for now, and had pocketed the rolled up funeral money from each of the sixth chambers. He was impressed with the ease of loading the Peacemaker, and again he wanted to shoot it, even while knowing that such a test would come only at a desperate last stand.

Carver had gone to the northern side. He gathered his men around him and gave what must be final instructions. Dowland looked south and saw a similar talk being led by a tall fellow with a lengthy moustache flying away from both sides of his face. Porterhouse, as Dowland dubbed him, was more animated in giving his orders, and from the general effect of his movements, Dowland could tell that a group of five men were to climb up the southern flank. Carver was likely giving the same order on the northern side.

The first assault began, and he felt a moment of sorrow for the men moving toward him. Carver and Porterhouse stood conspicuously out of range. He lay down on the dome with his feet pointed westward and his arms resting on its high point. He aimed first at the northern group. They had gone with Carver, and shooting them felt something like a mercy.

Dowland waited until the men were a quarter of the way up before he took his first shot. He fired once and worked the lever. The leading man stopped and fell backward. Dowland fired at the second. Both now tumbled, shoving the other three off their feet and sending the lot of them, the quick and the dead, sliding.

He swung his rifle over toward the southern flank, but the men climbing that side had already turned tail and were running and falling and running again. They were almost too far away already, and their haphazard progress made a predictable shot increasingly difficult.

The discussions that ensued on both sides of the mesa were more lively than the previous ones. The men showed an altogether uncooperative attitude toward a second attempt. The shrugged their shoulders and waved their arms toward the mesa, all the while inching away. In a fury, Carver slapped the two of them who were in reach.

Porterhouse, on the other hand, must have realized that he had just obeyed Carver's order and would not be able to follow another without going around the mesa to hear it. He looked to be forming his own plan, one that seemed to be rising from some intelligence. Four of his men had rifles, and he motioned for them to go to the southern flank. He then pointed first at the eastern slope and then at four other men, presumably armed only with revolvers.

Dowland shot a glance at Carver, wondering if the sheriff would send his men on another attempt. If he did, he would be facing an approach from all three sides. While he waited, he pulled two cartridges out of the box and loaded them into his rifle.

He covered the southern approach first, as Carver's men were already spooked, and the men with rifles were the greatest danger for the moment.

They moved toward the mesa cautiously. When they reached the flank, they crouched low and stayed on the eastern side of the flying buttress of rock that worked its way up to the top. They stopped about halfway up.

The other four made their way to the eastern slope and up into the trees. They began their climb, and the four on the southern flank fired. Shots whistled above him, and two struck the dome only a couple of feet away from his head. He lay flat for a moment, listening to the pattern. The riflemen were firing slowly. Their job was to keep his head down while the men with revolvers moved closer.

Dowland felt the rhythm of the rifle shots, and once he had felt enough, he lifted up slightly during a pause and returned two of his own. One connected. A rifle clattered down the side of the mesa, its owner lying dead.

A rapid series of cracks drew his attention toward the trees. The four men among them fired wildly, hitting the trees mostly, but a few bullets broke through to burn past Dowland. He saw a flash in the branches and rose a bit to take a shot. He dropped down just before three bullets from the rifles passed through the point where his head had been. The blood pounded in his ears, but as his heart calmed, he heard a man groaning among the trees and three separate rustling noises hurrying down the slope. The rifles had also stopped firing. He rose up again, hoping to get another shot at the riflemen, but they were already down the side and too far away.

A bullet glanced off the rock and passed him so close that he felt the air parting over his head. The shot had come from the northern side. He flattened against the dome and waited a moment before rising up again and taking another shot. This one missed, but it was close enough to send those men scrambling back down the way that they had come.

Dowland sat up and contemplated his situation. Seventeen men remained on the flat land surrounding the mesa. They grouped together around Carver or Porterhouse and looked to be at a loss as to what to do. They must have realized that they were at a stalemate. Several of the men in each group lighted fires and settled in. This time, the sheriff made no objection.

By the moon, he saw that it was past midnight. It was quiet, all but for the groans of the man lying among the trees.

Dowland thought about going down to help him, but he knew that if he left the dome, Carver would immediately send a new assault. He stood up.

"Sheriff Carver," he called out, "you have a man down here in the trees. He's still alive, if that matters to you."

"And I suppose you're offering us safe passage on your mountain," Carver shouted back. "Why don't you just bring him to us? That would make things easier for all concerned."

"That's the second time that you've made me out to be a fool. Don't plan on a third. On your head be your man's life."

Dowland watched Carver's men and saw the discontent that he was trying to brew.

The night settled into a weary passage. Carver shouted for a while, then paced between two large rocks on the far side of his men. Eventually he gathered up Patterson and Oakes from beside the fire and shoved them forward. Dowland wondered if they were going to try their own assault until he realized that the sheriff was heading for Porterhouse.

The five remaining on the northern side were slow to appreciate their new circumstances. They poked at the fire and drank coffee. One of them smoked. Carver and company had reached Porterhouse by the time the five realized that they were alone. Dowland contemplated offering them some leaden encouragement, but there was no need, as furtively and one by one, the men sneaked away. There were now only twelve to his one.

Or was it thirteen? The man in the trees continued to groan. He was no threat, but he was an irritation. Dowland was on the edge of going to him, but he looked again toward Carver and saw the sheriff standing with Porterhouse several yards from his men. The sheriff reached into his pocket, pulled out a cigar, and lighted it. From the glow of the fire that the men were sitting around, Dowland could see the smoke rising a bit before being carried away westward by the wind that blew gently across the flat land.

Porterhouse had been speaking, but as he looked at the cigar, his mouth stopped moving, and he stared. He must have realized something, for he began stabbing his finger back and forth between the eastern slope of the mesa and the sheriff.

Carver finally understood what Porterhouse was saying to him. He ran over to his men, and after kicking two of them, got them into motion. The lot of them collected their weapons and hurried toward the slope.

Dowland did not know what they were about to do, but he moved down to the bottom of the dome and a little into the trees. There was one place on the edge where he had a good shot at anyone who came close enough from the southern side.

He waited, barely breathing, his rifle aimed steadily at the base of the mesa. He caught glimpses of movement out of the corner of his right eye, but he did not turn his head or move his gaze. Quiet had fallen on the dome. The man in the trees was no longer groaning. The only sound was the susurration of the trees in the wind.

Carver and his men came into the line of sight. Dowland held until enough of them were visible. At this range, he needed several targets for his bullets to connect. Finally, he fired five rapid shots.

Two bodies lay on the ground. He was now opposed by just ten foes, and he laughed for a moment. If this hand-ful was the total number of his enemies, he had become altogether too well liked.

He climbed to the top of the dome to see what Carver was trying now, and his cheerful humor drained. The scent of wood smoke sharpened the air, and flashes of light pierced through the branches. Porterhouse had set fires.

A blaze grew and swept forward across the mesa. He ran from one side of the dome to the other, but a fringe of stubby junipers surrounded the bare rock, and the tonsure would not be enough to save him. He had one chance: the shelf on the western edge.

But before he could move, shots burst out from the trees, and his right arm went numb. A sheen of red grew along the sleeve and sparkled in the moonlight. His rifle dropped to the ground. With his left hand, he pulled the Peacemaker and fired into the advancing wall of flame. After four rounds, then cursed himself for being a fool. He was shooting at a dead man's gun.

He ran across the dome, heading for the shelf, but the loose rock gave way, and his feet flew out from under him. He slid down the rock and through the brush, steering himself as best he could. The sky spread out before him.

Grasping at what little remained, he reached out his left arm and hooked it around one of the trees clinging to the edge. He stopped short, but the Peacemaker flew on.

Dowland hung on the edge of the mesa's wall. The shelf was five irksome yards to his right. His left arm was only sore, though, not broken or dislocated. His right had begun to ache. He pulled himself upward by bracing his feet against the tree and pulling on another with his left hand. He wanted to rest, but the flames racing around the dome and the air thickening with smoke refused him the time for that.

Going from tree to tree, he worked his way over toward the shelf, then dropped down onto it and huddled against the wall as the fire engulfed the mesa. The wind roared overhead, shooting gusts of flame outward and carrying blazing masses of sticks and leaves into open air. He was chilled by the updraft that mounted the wall to inspire the conflagration.

Pressing against the rock, he checked his right arm. The bullet had missed the bone. The ragged wound was shallow. It would need sewing up, but that had to wait. He took out his knife and cut away the sleeve for a bandage. He wrapped his arm, tying a loose knot that he tightened with the aid of his teeth, and lowered himself to rest.

At his waist were his two friends, Alpha and Omega. He turned around and pushed himself out to the end of the shelf, then lay back facing the dome. The top was just visible. His mind wandered back to the night that his dormitory burned during his senior year at the College of William and Mary. He had been cold then too, standing in the winter air in his night shirt and watching the tongues of fire outshine the stars.

Dowland rested Omega in his left hand across his stomach and pondered the strange beauty of the fire that burned above him, filling the sky with light.

He awoke to see a new light above him. The sun was rising, and its rays shimmered through the swirling smoke. His left arm ached, and his right arm had a dull soreness, but he was alive, and pain was the price of living.

He heard movement and voices above him. Two men were picking their way through the burned trees toward the dome.

"Here's what's left of his rifle," one of them said.

"But nothing of him," Carver answered.

Dowland stood and aimed Omega toward the top of the dome. He would get one shot. The first voice must belong to Porterhouse, and he wondered if he ought to take his shot at the brains of the operation or its evil heart.

Fate brought Porterhouse to the top first. Dowland hesitated, wanting the sheriff, but Porterhouse saw him and swung his rifle around toward the shelf. Dowland fired true, and Porterhouse shot wildly as he fell dead.

"So here we are," Carver called out from beyond the top of the dome. "You're still trapped on this mesa, and from the looks of the ashes up here, you have no food and no water. My men and I can wait. How long do you have?"

"Long enough, Carver," Dowland shouted back. "Whether by my bullets or your folly, you keep losing men. Give it a few hours, and there will just be the two of us."

A shower of rocks fell at Dowland, and he dived for cover against the wall.

"I have enough to make your life unpleasant," Carver yelled. More rocks came down.

"You do that yourself."

Carver said nothing in return, but Dowland heard several men straining on the dome. Wondering what new torment Carver was working, he heard a series of crashes. A boulder then slammed into the shelf and teetered for a moment before falling off. There was a crack beneath his feet.

Dowland shoved Omega back into his belt and clung to the rock face. Another boulder plummeted down. On impact, it took the shelf with it. He pressed his face against the rock, not wanting to see the shelf hit the ground a hundred feet below. It struck with a heavy thud.

He looked up to see Carver standing on the edge looking down at him. Carver jumped back for a moment, but then reappeared.

"So you've been shot, I see. Interesting choice before you – hold on for your life or shoot me as you fall." Carver stepped back. "Men, go fetch that barrel of powder and some rope. We've got a prairie dog to blast out."

Dowland heard the men making their way through the burned trees down the mesa's slope. Carver's suggestion seemed a fitting end to this battle, and he studied the idea of pushing himself away from the cliff wall, pulling out Omega, and firing, all done rapidly enough to hit the sheriff, but the sound of someone coming back up the slope shifted his attention.

Carver heard the sound as well. He did not turn to look, but instead stood at the edge, staring down. "Here come my men," he said smugly. "Have you decided?"

"Not your men," a voice called out from the top of the dome. It was Morrison.

Carver tensed, then slumped forward, and fell.

This time Dowland watched the falling body's path to the bottom, and as he did so, his ears registered the shot.

"Can you climb up?" Morrison asked, now standing where the sheriff had been.

"I'll tell you when I've done it." He inched his way up by lifting himself with his legs and steadying himself with his left hand and elbow. When he was high enough, Morrison reached down and helped him the rest of the way. "What about the sheriff's men?" Dowland asked once safely on the mesa.

"They saw me coming and ran."

66

"And there's Carver, shot in the back and splayed out on the ground below us," Dowland said.

"A fitting end," Morrison replied.

"Perhaps, but at such a cost."

"At least I can bury my wife in peace now, thanks to you, and my boy's safe."

"Oh, yes, young Henry," Dowland said as the two of them climbed the dome. "Take me to see my namesake."

The End

Kenneth Newton –

Kenneth Newton writes out of Ridgecrest, California. He is a student of the Civil War and the Westward Expansion, and he combines these elements in much of his fiction.

His stories have been accepted by literary magazines including *Writers West, The New Southern Literary Messenger, Unknowns,* and *Bane K. Wilker's Tales of the Old West.*

His post-Civil War novel, *Passing Through Kansas,* will be available in 2012 from AuthorHouse.

APACHE GOLD

Kenneth Newton

Sgt. Sam Gage stopped his mount alongside Capt. Harlan Drake's horse. "Cap'n, you reckon we might git lucky enough to find the gold and git gone without runnin' into that big Injun?"

"That would be OK with me, Sam," Drake replied, studying his map. "But right now I'm more worried about Yanks. I think we're already a lot closer to Fort Craig than I want to be. When we clear these hills, we'll bear southwest and put those mountains between us and the fort." He rolled the map and scanned the countryside. "But Milagro could be anywhere out here."

The remnants of Troop B, First Texas Volunteer Cavalry, were in a high desert valley with scattered patches of prairie grass, dotted with clumps of pinion pine and juniper shrubs. They were trying to stay close enough to the hills to be seen, but far enough away to avoid an ambush.

Sgt. Gage spoke up. "Ya figger that 'pache will take us fer soldiers in these rags?"

Drake had to agree that in his tattered gray tunic with its faded gold piping, he only slightly resembled a uniformed soldier. He wore a Confederate cavalry officer's hat and sported the requisite beard. He had lived his life clean-shaven before the war, but there were things that took too much time and effort for a soldier more than two years in the field, and shaving was one of them. The gray whiskers made him look older than his years, but he was long past worrying about such things.

In their butternut homespuns, his men looked more like hard-scrabble farmers, save for the makeshift stripes on their sleeves. "He'll know we're soldiers. He would've seen the stars and bars, or something similar, back in '62." He glanced up at the white flag high above Sgt. Gage's head. "And we know he's come in to talk under a white flag before. Let's hope he's willing to do it again, because he's bound to have us outnumbered. According to Colonel Becker, O'Kelly counted a good forty warriors and a village of around two hundred all together."

Drake's conversation with Lieutenant Colonel Ellis Becker had taken place more than three months before and a good 2,000 miles away. Drake had been summoned to the colonel's tent at their winter encampment near the Shenandoah Valley. "Captain," Becker said, warming his hands at his small stove, "it's no secret the Confederacy is strapped. It's near impossible to fight defensively, let along wage a campaign. There's damn little forage to be found, and we're running short of everything from ammunition to shoes."

"Yes, sir," Drake said, "including payroll."

Becker arched his brow. "You and your Texans are being paid every month, according to the paymaster, just like everyone else attached to my Division."

"True enough, sir, and we're not mercenaries, but everybody knows those Confederate shinplasters are next to worthless. I hear a pair of half-decent boots is two hundred dollars in Richmond. A trooper's thirteen dollars a month won't go far at that rate."

"Do yourself a favor and save those shinplasters, Capt. Drake. I guarantee you when this war is over, they will be accepted and highly-valued not only in this country, but around the world. But, having said that, your point is well taken." Becker handed Drake a cheroot as he seated himself and motioned for Drake to sit. "General Lee and President Davis are convinced, as am I, that the good folks up north will soon lose their stomach for this fight and convince old Abe to call it off. So, starting in the spring, we need to hit them hard – inflict heavy casualties. But we need supplies, or more to the point, the means to pay for supplies from overseas, and to prod the merchants to risk running the blockade. That's where you come in, Captain."

Drake managed a thin smile as he leaned forward to accept the light Becker offered him. "Well, I'm afraid I'm a little short right now, sir." He puffed the cigar to life. "Thanks. I guess I miss an occasional good smoke about as much as I miss anything these days."

"I'll personally see to it you're kept in honest-to-God Havanas for the rest of your life if you succeed in this operation."

Drake leaned back in the chair. "Well, sir, then I guess it's about time I found out just what it is you want me to do."

"You'll recall," began the colonel, "that we took a few prisoners at Cedar Creek before the tide turned and we had to fall back."

As he motioned his little column forward, Drake wished

for the hundredth time they'd let those Yankees go, and he'd never heard of this "operation." Becker went on to explain that after spending two months in Libby Prison, one of the Federals managed to get himself brought before the prison commander. In exchange for his release, one Sgt. Michael O'Kelly offered to deliver to the Confederacy a fortune in Union gold. The camp commander had at first listened to the preposterous tale in weary amusement, but came to believe O'Kelly might be telling the truth and relayed the story up the chain of command. It made its way back down the chain as far as Lt. Col. Becker, in the form of a note that said simply:

Jubal – War Dept recommends we pursue this matter soonest. I concur. Use your best judgment, and Godspeed. Signed, R. E. Lee.

Jubal was Jubal Early, Commanding General of the Army of Northern Virginia's II Corps, who had personally delivered the note to Becker for action. Drake's assignment was to mount an expedition to New Mexico and retrieve the gold for the Confederacy.

Becker's tone was slightly apologetic. "We're in desperate straits, Captain. Desperate men must of necessity engage in acts of desperation."

Becker would give him only twenty men. "It's regrettable," he said, "but General Early was adamant that he couldn't commit a larger force to this mission. Regrettable, but convenient for me, because that's about how many men you currently have at your disposal, and your twenty are as good as any twenty I've got. I'm not sure Early believes this is worth doing, but like you and me, he has his orders.

"However, you'll have the best horses, mules, and equipment I can find." Becker hesitated. "And, uh, oh yes — a

Gatling gun."

"A Gatling gun, sir?"

"Yes, we captured one at Lynchburg." He made a cranking motion with his right hand. "It's that wheeled rapid-fire contraption the some of the Union Infantry Divisions drag around but don't seem to ever use."

"I've heard of it, sir, and what I've heard is that it's a barely- functional weapon, more trouble than it's worth."

The colonel sighed. "It's true they tend to jam, and aren't suitable for typical battlefield conditions. But I'm hoping it might impress this heathen Milagro into cooperating."

"I'm half afraid to ask at this point, Colonel, but who's Milagro?"

In late fall of 1862, according to Sgt. O'Kelly, the commander of the Federal army garrison at Denver, Maj. Thomas Reed, had found himself short of troops when most of his regulars were abruptly withdrawn to fight the rebels in the east. The few misfits, malcontents, and irregulars still at his disposal were barely adequate to maintain the garrison, let alone escort a number one priority, top secret shipment to Col. Edward Canby at Fort Craig in New Mexico. He elected to transport the shipment on a caisson normally used for hauling ammunition, in hopes that the handful of men he could spare to send on the mission would look like just another routine patrol. Even though his orders were to deliver it in no more than ten days without fail, Reed professed ignorance as to the contents of the sealed iron strongbox. Nonetheless, by the time the escort was selected and ready to leave, the garrison was alive with the rumor that the heavy box contained king's ransom in gold bullion.

Sgt. O'Kelly and his nondescript caisson were less than

a day from Fort Craig when some twenty or thirty Mexican bandits encountered the convoy. Whether they were aware of the contents of the caisson or just wanted the weapons and horses, no one knew. But the bandits ambushed the soldiers near Socorro, killing all but one. Sgt. O'Kelly was taken alive as future trading stock, and the bandits began a hasty retreat for the border, certain the gringo *federales* would soon be out in force and on their trail.

Two days later, as they nursed the caisson through a narrow mountain pass in the Organ Mountains, the Mexicans were in turn set upon and slaughtered by a party of Mescalero Apaches led by a war chief O'Kelly would come to know as Milagro. The sergeant was thrown from his mount during the melee, and with his hands tied behind his back, had landed hard and been knocked senseless. His eyes focused just in time for him to see Milagro stay the hand of the warrior who was about to crush his skull with a stone war club.

Milagro knelt down and roughly grabbed a handful of O'Kelly's tunic, hauling him up until they were nose to nose. "Habla espanol?" asked the Apache. Milagro knew that very few white men would ever bother to learn the language of the Apache, but some could make the Mexican words. O'Kelly nodded that he did, and Milagro gestured toward the dead Mexicans. "Que paso?"

O'Kelly told the Apache about the ambush at Socorro as one of the warriors brought over a heavy golden ingot for Milagro to see.

Milagro nodded. "The thing that makes the white men and Mexicans crazy," he said, then turned back to O'Kelly. "So the banditos thought if more bluecoats came, you would be of use. Will the soldiers come for you and this box of gold?"

"To be sure. Hundreds of them and soon."

Milagro shoved him roughly to the ground. "Hundreds!" he spat. "There are not one hundred, and I know it. First you fought with the Mexicans, then you fought the other white soldiers – the graycoats – and all the time you were fighting the Apache, too. No one can fight so much for so long and have hundreds of men, and those you do have are running away. I have seen it, and I know it is so. The bluecoats drove out the graycoats, and now the Apache have driven the bluecoats from Apache land! Soon there will be no more of you. Hundreds! Why do you lie?"

O'Kelly was unsure how to deal with the Apache's notion that the troop withdrawals signaled a retreat. "Well," he said, "there might not still be hundreds here, but they'll be along for me and the gold." He considered mentioning that back east there were not hundreds, nor thousands, but tens of thousands of bluecoats, but he feared the Indian would surely kill him in a fit of rage over a "lie" of that size. "We're still fighting the rebs – the graycoats. Not around here, any more, but far away." He pointed. "Back east."

Milagro put a knife to O'Kelly's throat. "And now you want me to believe the soldiers who fled from the Apache have only gone to fight the other white men? Still you lie."

"Well, I meant some of them went to fight the graycoats. Most of them ran away from the Apache."

Milagro put pressure on the tip of the blade. This white man would say whatever it was he thought a man with a knife wanted to hear. He applied pressure until the blade made a small scratch on the white man's throat and shook his head in disgust as the bluecoat yelped in pain. Milagro stood and walked away, crooking a finger at the warrior who still stood over the enemy soldier, war club poised to strike. "Bring him," he said.

Sgt. Gage pulled up and dropped back to regain his position in the column. As he looked for signs of life in the forbidding landscape, Drake asked himself the same question he had asked Col. Becker. "Why me?"

"Because you speak Spanish, for one thing, which is a fairly rare commodity in my Division, and also because I know your pedigree, Captain. You served with Sam Houston during the war for Texas independence, you fought in the Mexican War, and then you chased outlaws with the Texas Rangers. Happily, you're also experienced in dealing with Indians – talking when you can and fighting when you have to, even if your area of expertise is Comanche." The colonel paused in the middle of Drake's resume to catch his breath. "But you didn't sign on with Sibley for the Western Campaign in '62. That was rather uncharacteristic of a gladiator like you, Captain Drake."

"I'm no gladiator. It just seems like ever since I was a boy there's been something going on in Texas that was important enough to fight about. But I couldn't see the point in going to New Mexico."

"Jeff Davis could. He believed possession of New Mexico could lead to further Confederate acquisitions in the west."

"Well, Colonel, that made about as much sense to me as seceding from the Union in the first place."

"Ah, yes. Find a way to compromise. A Sam Houston man to the end."

"I suppose I am, plus I had a cattle ranch to look after. Still do, I hope. And to be truthful, I didn't think the

Confederacy was going to need my help."

Becker nodded. "A lot of us thought it was going to be a short fight." He paused as if to reflect on the magnitude of that particular miscalculation. "We've all suffered losses of one kind or another, Captain, and I sincerely hope your ranch is there waiting for you when you get home. But the secession wasn't about whether you were doing well in San Antonio, or whether I was fat, dumb, and happy in Virginia. It was about the fact that every new western state added to the Union was going to be a nail in the coffin of the southern states. Several nails, really, in the form of two senators and God knows how many congressmen who might well be expected to vote one day to abolish slavery in the United States of America, thereby impoverishing every state south of the Mason and Dixon line. Some will cite other reasons besides slavery, and they're real enough. But absent the so-called 'peculiar institution,' the southern states had no viable future in the Union, and you know that, as well as I do."

Drake crossed to the door of the tent, drawing aside the flap to look outside at the heavy grayness of the bleak, dormant landscape. "Well, sir," he said, "here's something I know. I never laid claim to ownership of another man, and never would. But if we made this fight over slavery, one day we're going to have to answer to Almighty God for it."

"It's a bit late for those sentiments, Captain. Old Abe has made a big show of freeing the slaves, to rub our noses in it. Both sides crossed the Rubicon some time ago. There's no turning back now."

Drake let the flap fall and turned to face Becker. "No, I suppose not."

"I gather that when Canby ran Sibley out of New Mexico,

you changed your mind about this fight."

"I did. Sibley was an acquaintance of mine, and his men were friends and neighbors – even relatives, some of them – and they came back in pretty rough shape. We raised a troop of cavalry, looking to go back out to New Mexico, and wound up here. But understand this, Colonel. I make no secret of the fact that my allegiance is to Texas. For better or worse, Texas has thrown in with the Confederacy. I've stood shoulder to shoulder with you Virginians from Chancellorsville to Gettysburg to Cedar Creek. But hell, I'm damn near fifty years old. Besides, I get seasick. If the boat ride to Galveston doesn't kill me, the ride across Texas will." He turned back toward Becker. "Much as I'd like the stogies, you need a younger man for this job. And O'Kelly speaks Spanish – he could interpret for whoever you chose to send."

"I choose to send you and your cavalrymen," Becker said. "I know you've turned down promotions to stay with the men you brought here, and that kind of cohesiveness is important." The colonel sighed and continued. "And, well, about O'Kelly. Of course, the intent was that he guide the expedition, but the fact is we no longer have him. I guess he didn't really trust us to set him free in New Mexico, because he somehow overpowered his guard and escaped between Richmond and here. I expect by now he's been caught behind our lines and shot for a spy. But we have the maps he drew, and Major Reed's confidential orders regarding the shipment, which are what made his story believable in the first place. O'Kelly lived with the Apaches for six months, and we have detailed locations and descriptions of their camps, water holes, and even the cave where Milagro put the gold." Becker rubbed at his beard. "That name – Milagro – it has a

Spanish ring to it."

Drake nodded. "It means miracle. Used as a man's name, I reckon it would mean he's a fella that's a cut or two above a normal man. Whoever hung that moniker on him believes this Apache has powerful medicine."

Becker chuckled. "Well, this miracle man is apparently quite the sport. After six months, he told O'Kelly he was tired of looking at him and turned him loose, just like that. Told him to go get his hundreds of long knife buddies and come back and get the gold, if they had the *cojones* for the job. Much to the sergeant's surprise, Canby was singularly uninterested in undertaking such an expedition, and the next thing O'Kelly knew, he was in the eastern theater."

Drake sat staring at his boots. "Lucky for me, I guess. It seems odd Canby wouldn't go after the gold."

"Yes, it does. And for all we know, he might well have gone and got it after O'Kelly was transferred. Maybe he wanted to wait until after the war and finish off the Apaches first, so he wouldn't have to fight his way to that cave. Or maybe it was so hush-hush that Canby didn't even know what was in the shipment and didn't believe O'Kelly. I don't know. Look, Captain. The War Department has been over and over and around and around this thing. They think this is a trip worth taking."

"Any suggestions as to how I go about claiming this gold for the cause?"

"Any way you can. Negotiate, offer a treaty on behalf of the Confederacy. Tell the Apaches we'll see to it the bluecoats don't bother them any more, we'll run the settlers and Mexicans out. Hell, tell this Milagro anything you have to, and promise him the moon. Failing that, I'm sure you're aware Congress has authorized discretionary extermination of hostiles as required. I don't care if you have to kill every warrior, squaw, and papoose in New Mexico. Your orders are to do whatever you have to do to get that gold."

Drake shook his head; Lt. Col. Becker hadn't done much Indian fighting, as simple as he made it sound. Just roll out the ol' Gatling gun and exterminate the lot of 'em, end of report. "As I recall, Sibley's orders in '62 were to run the Federals out of New Mexico, and then carry on as appropriate, using his own good judgment. If I have the same leeway, why don't I just go ahead and take California while I'm out there? It seems a shame to take a half a platoon of cavalry that far and not finish the job."

Becker flared. "God damn it, Captain, I know!" he shouted, then just as quickly calmed down. "I know. But we simply have no choice. We have to try."

Drake nodded. "Sorry, I was out of line."

"Never mind, and by the way, you won't have to worry about seasickness. The blockade is too formidable. The odds of making Galveston would be remote."

Drake sighed heavily, somehow not surprised. Of course, the Navy wouldn't risk a valuable blockade runner on a job such as this.

Becker walked across the tent and put a hand on Drake's shoulder. "I know you could simply lead your men home to San Antonio and forget all about this unpleasantness, but I know you won't. You have quite a ride ahead of you, Captain, and you need to get started. Every day is precious to the Confederacy."

"Riders comin, Cap'n!" Gage was alongside again, offering Drake his binoculars. "I think we found us some 'paches."

Through the field glasses Drake could make out the shimmering image of six men riding abreast at a slow gallop. Just out of rifle range they stopped, and one man continued at a trot, a white flag held above his head on the end of a lance.

"Give me your truce flag, Sergeant," Drake said as he jerked a thumb over his shoulder toward the rear of the column. "Unhitch that gun and get it ready to use." Six days earlier they'd assembled the Gatling gun, and they were now pulling it behind the stout mule that had packed it all the way from Virginia.

The old sergeant was used to barking orders. "Simmons, Getusky! Break out that gun! Everybody dismount and take cover as best you can, and wait for orders!" Turning back to Drake, he said, "I wouldn't go out there by m'self, Cap'n. A man shouldn't trust a injun with his life."

The Indian continued to advance alone. "He seems to trust us," Drake said, "and I won't get any closer to his men than he gets to mine." He nodded toward the pair of pommel holsters slung across his saddle, each of which held a .44 caliber Colt's Dragoon revolver. "These horse pistols have seen me through a few scrapes in nigh on twenty years. I'll be all right. But if anything happens to me, the most important thing is to complete the mission, and get the boys out of here." He handed Gage the oilskin pouch. "If the location of the cave is as accurate as everything else on these maps, it's no more than half a day southwest of here. And if the mountain looks anything like O'Kelly's sketch, you shouldn't have any trouble finding it." He unholstered the revolvers and checked the loads, put them away, and turned back to Gage. "If there's any gold to be had, Sergeant, you can't leave here

81

without it, no matter if I'm dead or alive. Is that understood?"

Gage scowled, but nodded. "Me'n the boys only got to run a few rounds through that gun back in Virginny, but we damn sure know how to make her spit lead. If'n that savage tries somethin, there'll be hell to pay. But I wisht I'd never heard tell of that damn gold."

Drake almost smiled. "Well, as someone once said to me, it's a bit late for those sentiments. We're soldiers. We'll do our job or die trying. If anything happens to me, you're in charge, and you're to get that gold and deliver it into the Confederacy's hands. That's an order, Sgt. Gage."

Drake urged his mount in the direction of the lone rider. The big bay gelding was bone tired and didn't want to so much as trot, but he was game, and he grudgingly headed out at a canter toward the advancing Apache.

The two men stopped when they were fifty feet apart, and then, as if on cue, each nudged his horse forward at a walk. When they stopped again, their horses were muzzle to muzzle. They studied each other in silence broken only by an occasional snort from one of their mounts.

The Indian was the younger man, no more than thirty-five, and tall for an Apache, with straight black hair that hung down his back past his shoulder blades. He wore a blue bandana around his head, tied at the back, and a red calico shirt with buckskin breeches and a white cotton breechclout. His moccasined feet were in the stirrups of a McClellan saddle that was covered with a gray woolen blanket. He held his lance in his left hand, and the buttstock of a Henry repeater protruded from a U.S. Army saddle scabbard beneath his right leg.

His dark eyes betrayed no fear or emotion of any kind as he sized up the tall and wiry graycoat soldier with the faded coat and brown trousers. Milagro knew white soldiers would lie beneath their peace rag. They always did, no matter the color of their uniforms. But in his experience, they wouldn't start a fight until after they had made their demand and been refused. Then they would go away and come back later with more men, ready to fight.

"Buenos dias," Drake said. "I have been sent by the chief of the graycoat soldiers to speak with Milagro."

The Apache straightened in the saddle. "I am the one the Mexicans call Milagro." The white man was dirty from head to toe. His pale blue eyes were set deep in his head, with long lines at the corners, and his horse was exhausted. "You have come a long way," said Milagro. "Have you finished your fight with the bluecoats, and come back to fight the Apache?"

"I come as a friend, to make peace, now and forever, between the graycoats and the Apache. My name is Harlan Drake. I'm a captain in the graycoat army." He transferred the white flag to his left hand and extended his right.

The Indian frowned and made no move to accept the hand. "I have met only two white men who wanted to be a friend to the Apache, and other white men killed them both. What does your chief want from me?"

Drake cleared his throat. "The bluecoats are your enemy, and ours. You have something that is of no use to you, and the graycoat soldiers need it to continue to fight our common enemy. It will be good for both of us when we defeat the bluecoats. My chief has sent me for the gold."

Milagro arched a brow. "What gold?"

"The gold the Mexicans took from the bluecoats and you

took from the Mexicans. O'Kelly was sent back east to fight in the big fight. We captured him and he told us you have it."

The Indian sneered. "O'Kelly! That one is a coward who would betray his mother to save himself. But if I have this gold, you have not told me why I should give it to you."

"After we defeat the bluecoats, we will burn their forts and make the white settlers leave, and give Apache land back to the Apaches. We'll punish the Mexicans and Commanches for raiding here." Drake could see that Milagro wasn't impressed by his speech, and he wasn't surprised. He didn't think much of it himself. "Hell, the truth is, you may be better off if the graycoats win the war, but I can't promise you a thing. I was sent to get the gold any way I can. I don't want to, but I'll fight you for it if I have to." He decided to play his trump card. "We have a new gun that you can't defeat. With it, one man can kill every Apache in an afternoon."

The Apache people had few friends; Milagro would have been willing to accept Drake as an honest enemy, but then came the lie about the gun. He gripped the butt of the Henry. "This gun can kill more men than the soldiers' guns, but it cannot do what you say. I have never seen such a gun."

"It's not a rifle. That's it over there, on wheels like a cannon. I don't want a fight, Milagro. If I show you that the gun will do what I say, will you let me take the gold and go in peace?" Drake knew the offer was a gamble. The Gatling gun might fire all day, but it was just as likely to misfeed and jam every five rounds.

Milagro shook his head. "If you have a gun that will do what you say, I will trade the gold for it."

Milagro stopped in mid sentence, and both men looked to

the west, their attention drawn there by the pounding hooves and rattling sabres of a small Union cavalry patrol as its vanguard topped a rise a quarter mile away. The eight or ten troopers fanned out along the ridge and stopped as their dust came up from behind and enveloped them.

Milagro trained a livid glare on Drake, who raised his hands in supplication. "They're no friends of mine."

Both men sat motionless in the saddle and watched as a single rider emerged from the dust and loped toward them, a white flag in the air above his head. Drake looked to his men. As Sgt. Gage had ordered, they had dismounted and taken what cover they could find, mostly behind small boulders and bushes. Gage, Simmons, and Getusky were more exposed, out front manning the Gatling gun, which looked to be set up and ready to fire. Milagro's companions sat stock-still on their ponies, watching and waiting.

The young lieutenant reined in, his mount nearly perpendicular to the two men's animals. He smiled, showing even, white teeth. He was clean-shaven and handsome, with thick blond hair prominent at his ears and down his neck.

"Gentlemen," he said, "I hope I'm not interrupting anything." Neither man responded, and he went on. "I know this fellow to be Milagro, and I expect you must be Capt. Harlan Drake."

Drake was taken aback. "You have the advantage of me, Lieutenant. How do you know my name?"

The young man removed his right glove and extended the bare hand. "Forgive me, Captain. Lt. William Tyler, 2nd U. S. Cavalry. Say, does he speak English?"

Drake released the lieutenant's hand with a bemused grin. This proceeding was becoming increasingly bizarre by the moment. He looked to Milagro and asked, "Habla ingles?" The Apache turned his head to the side and spat.

"I'd take that to be a no. And I'll ask again how you know me."

"I not only know who you are, I know why you're here," the young man replied. "You and I need to talk, Captain." He glanced from side to side. "Preferably somewhere in the shade, if there's any shade to be found around here . . . ."

Lt. Tyler's voice trailed off and his eyes stopped their search. He was distracted by a puff of smoke from atop a rocky hillside behind and above the Confederate position. His eyes widened in surprise as the bullet arrived just ahead of the report, thudding loudly into his abdomen above the navel.

Drake's mount started and reared, and in so doing put itself in the path of the second slug. The gelding flinched violently when the bullet struck its neck, and stumbled slightly as its front hooves regained the ground, but the beleaguered warhorse didn't fall. Another bullet hissed over-head as Milagro wheeled his pony about and kicked it into a gallop. The Apache hunkered low over his horse's withers as he sped away toward his companions.

Drake cursed his foul luck as sporadic shooting erupted from the blue and gray ranks. The distance between the two forces was too great for either side to do wholesale damage to the other; he and the boy, meanwhile, were in no man's land, and well within range of a stray round from either direction. Lt. Tyler put his hand to his stomach and pulled it slowly away, staring incredulously at the crimson stain on his palm. He trained a bewildered glare on Drake, silently demanding an explanation for the treachery that had wounded him.

Drake snatched up the lieutenant's reins as the staccato bark of the Gatling gun joined the rifle fire. "Oh, Christ!" he muttered. Things were rapidly going to hell, and the Gatling gun was showing the way. There was a sizable clump of rocks, perhaps two hundred yards away in the direction of the near foothills, and the immediate problem was to get himself and Lt. Tyler some cover. As he urged his bleeding horse forward, Drake saw that Sgt. Gage had the gun trained not on the Yankees or Indians, but on the hillside behind them. The heavy bullets were lifting chunks of earth and rock into the air and splintering foliage, but Drake couldn't see any sign of a rifleman in the midst of the hail of slugs.

Apparently satisfied with the work he'd done on the hill, Gage ordered the gun wheeled about. The Apaches had vanished, so he directed fire on the Union line. Drake was raising a hand to call the sergeant off when his dying horse stumbled and fell. Unhorsed, he lost his hold on the white flag and Tyler's reins, and the panicked animal reared and threw the lieutenant as Gage opened up on the Federals. The bluecoats withdrew and dropped out of site behind the rise, but several quickly reappeared in prone position, leveling their carbines and firing at will as the Gatling gun peppered the ground in front of them.

Drake crawled to Tyler's side, and realized that at least some of the Union fire was directed at him. He managed to get himself and Tyler behind his fallen horse as bullets whined all around them. Two slugs struck the thrashing animal, and it heaved a final heavy sigh and became still as the firing tapered off. Drake rested a few seconds to catch his breath, and checked Tyler's wound. When he pressed he could feel the bullet with his finger; if the bleeding stopped, the boy might have a chance.

"Why did your man on the hill shoot me, Captain?" Lt. Tyler's tone was calm and matter-of-fact.

"I don't know who shot you, son, but it wasn't one of my men. Our problem right now, though, is that your men are shooting at us. We need to show them you're not dead."

"They're not too far wrong, are they? I'm gut-shot. I know what that means."

"Well, if it was me, I'd be a goner. But you've been eating better than me, and you're stronger. I think maybe the bullet's into nothing more than fat and muscle." Drake pressed a kerchief against the wound. "Here. You hold this, and I'll get that white flag up in the air again and call this off. Do you have a surgeon?"

Tyler swallowed hard. "At Fort Craig, yes. And my men should already be on their way there by now. They had orders to go for reinforcements if it came to a fight." He shook his head. "I never dreamed it would."

Drake could see no movement atop the rise. "You may be right."

A few minutes later Gage confirmed it as he galloped up and dismounted, excited and breathing heavily. "The 'paches and Yanks have all turned tail, Cap'n. That gun's a reg'lar corker. She's jammed up right now, but the boys'll have her goin' in a minute. Why, if'n we'd a had a dozen o' them at Gettysburg, we coulda showed them yanks a thing or two, I'll wager."

Half an hour later Lt. Tyler had his shady spot. They'd strung a tarpaulin between two pinion pines and put him on a blanket out of the sun, then given him the last of their laudanum and enough food and water to last until the patrol from Fort Craig came after him. His wound had stopped bleeding, and he was resting fairly comfortably when Drake knelt down beside him. "I'd like to have that talk now, Lieutenant, if you're up to it."

Tyler lifted his heavy lids and nodded. "I believe that's a good idea." He swallowed hard and continued. "They found a copy of your orders, maybe in Richmond, or maybe with one of your officers in the field. Most of the north and west is connected by telegraph now, Captain. They wired us some time ago that you might be on your way here or that you might have already come and gone. Then a few days ago, one of our Apache scouts spotted you, and they relayed the word to the fort. When they set out to deliver a message quickly, they can put the pony express to shame."

Drake didn't know what the pony express might be; he did know an Indian could travel light and fast when he wanted to. But he was more interested in goings-on back east. "Are you saying you've taken Richmond?"

The young man fixed his eyes on Drake's. "As I said, we have a lot to talk about. First of all, Captain, there is no gold out here, and never was. There was a shipment, all right. But all it's good for is making bullets and sinkers for fishing. It was just lead, made to look like gold. It's called fire gilding. Somehow or other they put a thin layer of real gold on the lead, and it sticks like skin."

Drake shook his head. "For what reason?"

"The shipment was a decoy. Details of it were intentionally let slip in Denver and Mexico and points in between. The idea was to draw attention to this shipment, in hopes the real gold shipment would go unnoticed."

Drake shook his head in disgust. "I hope somebody

needed that gold real bad."

"Well, they told us at West Point a leader sometimes has to make hard decisions. I trust the officer who decided to sacrifice those men has lost his share of sleep over it. Trouble was, there were rumors going around about sending gold to Mexico, and they were true. It was necessary to risk a handful of lives for a greater good." Tyler grimaced in pain, and took a deep breath before continuing. "The gold was bound for the war coffers of Mexican President Benito Juarez. The United States had formally recognized his government; he had ideas our government liked, including his opposition to slavery in Mexico. But he had enemies who were getting outside help, mainly from France, and he needed cash. The actual shipment went to California, then to Acapulco by sea. Juarez supposedly got it, but if he did, it didn't help him much, because Maximilian was in charge inside of six months." Tyler responded to Drake's puzzled expression. "He's the Austrian the French have made Emperor of Mexico."

Drake stood and walked a few steps away. In a single motion he removed his hat and wiped his brow with his sleeve, then he slapped the dusty hat against his leg. "I might have chewed tougher gristle," he said as he stared out across the desert, "though I can't say I remember when."

"There's more to choke down. Do you know what the date is, Captain Drake?"

Drake turned back toward Tyler. "I'd make it early June."

"It's Sunday, the fourth of June, 1865, to be precise. You were a while getting here."

"We travelled mostly at night, trying to avoid patrols. Hell, we laid up for days at a time, waiting for a chance to slip by a bunch of you all without trouble. Even so, we had four skirmishes, and I lost three men and two horses on the way. There's a war going on back there, Lieutenant. Or should I say there was a war going on?"

Tyler nodded. "General Lee surrendered on April ninth. For all practical purposes, the war's been over for nearly two months. Bring me my saddlebags, if you would."

When Drake handed him the bags, Tyler removed a folded newspaper and handed it over. Drake perused the paper in silence. The copy of the Denver Herald was dated April 15. "ASSASSINATION!" the huge headline read, and the sub-headline added, "President Lincoln Murdered. The Nation in Mourning." Drake nodded and returned the newspaper to Tyler, then went to talk with his men.

An hour later they were ready to leave, and Drake knelt down beside Tyler, who was looking at a small photograph. "Are you a family man, Captain?" he asked.

"No, I never seemed to find the time for all that."

Tyler showed him the picture of a raven haired young woman. "A man needs to make time. Our first is on the way. She's going to join me after the baby comes, as soon as they're able to travel. There's no finer thing than having a good woman and children at home."

Drake nodded. "I don't doubt that. I hope you understand I can't stay here with you. I'm not doing any more fighting, but I'll not see these men clamped in irons for six months while some desk major decides what to do with them." He breathed a heavy sigh. "If there was anything I could do for you, I'd send them home and stay with you, but –"

Tyler didn't make him finish the sentence. "I know, and I also know the grief that has befallen me is of my own doing.

I'm not your responsibility. There'll be a patrol out looking for me tomorrow. With luck they'll get here before the Apaches come back."

Drake put a hand on the lieutenant's shoulder. "What made you come out here with barely more than a squad in the first place? If you hadn't run into us, Milagro would have made short work of your patrol."

"I don't think so. The militia has been tough on him the last couple of years – worse than the regular army ever was. Their goal is extermination, and they waste no effort looking for a legal pretext to shoot Indians. The half dozen braves Milagro had with him are most likely all he's got left. My intent, if I ran into him, was to offer him a final chance to come to the fort and surrender and lead his people back to the reservation." Lt. Tyler closed his eyes and breathed deeply. "I didn't get out of West Point in time to fight in the war. I'm embarrassed to admit it, Captain, but the reason I brought my little volunteer patrol out here was to find you and accept the final surrender of the Civil War. I thought perhaps there might be room in the history books for a short paragraph on the subject. Instead, I may well become . . . . " His voice trailed off.

Drake knew what Lt. Tyler's footnote to history might be. He went to his mount and retrieved his saber, then walked back to kneel for a final time beside the young officer. "Lt. Tyler," he said, "I surrender. The Union can count on no more trouble from me." He held out the saber.

Tyler turned his head. "Thank you, Captain, but there is no need to humor me at this point."

"I'm not. I'm surrendering myself and the men under my command on the following conditions: that you not require us to stack our arms, that you let us be on our way with the animals presently in our possession, including your horse, and that you make our agreement known to the commanding officer at Fort Craig. I don't want a platoon following me to Texas looking for a fight."

Tyler took the saber. "Those conditions are acceptable, but I would require that you make certain the Gatling gun doesn't fall into Apache hands. Either disable the weapon, or take it with you."

Drake nodded. "Agreed. Good luck to you, son," he said, extending his hand.

Tyler gripped Drake's hand as firmly as he could. "And to you, sir."

"Two sets o' tracks, Cap'n, headin off to the southwest," Sgt. Gage said. "One set deeper'n the other, probl'y a horseman an a pack animal that ain't packin much. Beats me how I never hit him, all the lead I put into that hill."

"Even your Gatling gun won't shoot through solid rock," Drake replied. "I'm going to follow that trail and see who I find, Sergeant. Whether you and the boys come along is up to you. I've got no right to order you anywhere."

"You say it, we do it, same as always. But if'n there ain't no gold, an no more war, why not just go on home an be done with it? You don't owe that kid lieutenant no vengeance. Are you fergettin how many o' us them Yanks have put under?"

"I'm not forgetting anything. I'm not forgetting that one hundred forty-two men elected me Captain and followed me to Virginia, and there's seventeen left. I'm not likely to ever forget that. But the coward that shot that kid could just as easily have shot me. I'd like to think you'd be after him if he had."

Gage was offended. "Until my horse died under me, an my shoes fell off'n my feet, an then some. But that Yank ain't nothin to you like you are to me."

"I'll tell you what he is to me, Sergeant. He's a kid playing soldier, who should have had a chance to grow up. You and me, we'd give our left arms to be able to go back in time and skip this war. But he felt deprived because he missed out on the fight. The man that shot him did it for only one reason: in hopes we'd all kill each other off, or do a good enough job of it to give him time to get the gold and be gone. I want to see the look in his eyes when he finds out there isn't any gold. And then I'll kill him."

Following the ambusher's tracks, they found the mountain silhouetted against a reddish purple sky at sundown, the jagged features along the crest almost exactly as drawn by Sgt. O'Kelly. The mountain rose perhaps a thousand feet above the valley floor, and a clearly defined path snaked its way up the slope. They passed the night without fires, and in the morning Drake made ready to head up the trail alone.

Sgt. Gage protested in vain. "There might be a dozen of 'em up there."

"You can see the tracks as well as I can," Drake said, "and the map doesn't say anything about another way up. Besides, this is my fight. Just give me until sundown. If I'm not back, then do what you think best."

The pass narrowed quickly, and Drake soon found himself closely walled in by rocks and trees. Halfway up, he tied his horse beside the path and, throwing the pommel holsters and heavy revolvers over his shoulder, continued on foot. An hour later he came to a wide spot in the trail where two animals and a human had clearly spent the night. Drake reminded himself the man he sought had only gotten a two or three hour head start, and he drew the Colt from the holster at his left breast. He looked back the way he had come, breathing heavily, and could see nothing but mountainside. The bushwhacker would be cautious, for sure, but there was no way to look back down that winding trail and spot a pursuer who was more than fifty yards distant.

He walked on, comforted by the smooth walnut and steel of the revolver, taking a few steps, then stopping to rest. He didn't know when he might round a turn and find the cave, and he hoped his ragged breathing wasn't as loud to the rest of the world as it sounded to him.

Over the noise of his breathing he heard the nicker of a horse, followed immediately by the click of a cocking hammer somewhere behind and to the right of him. He put his thumb to the Colt's hammer spur.

"I wouldn't, Johnnie Reb. All I've gotta do is touch this trigger. You just holster that horse pistol, drop the lot, and keep on walkin, with your hands on top of your hat. Now!"

Drake did as he was told, feeling stupid and angry. He heard the bushwhacker drop to the ground behind him as he walked, and twenty paces later the path ended in a clearing. The horse and donkey were tied off to the right, and a small opening, roughly four feet square, disappeared darkly into the face of the granite. Twelve shiny golden rectangles, perhaps four by two by eight inches, were stacked on the ground near the entrance to the cave.

"A fine sight, hey, Johnnie? I swear I never thought you lot would actually come after it, though."

Drake looked at the ground. "I kinda thought it would turn out to be you, O'Kelly," he said.

95

O'Kelly walked by him, tossing the pommel holsters aside, a Spencer carbine trained on the center of Drake's heaving chest. "We had a deal, O'Kelly," Drake said. "That gold belongs to the Confederacy."

Michael O'Kelly was a big Irishman, over six feet tall, perhaps forty, with grizzled whiskers, red-nosed and paunchy. "But darlin," he laughed, "there *is* no Confederacy."

Drake didn't know what else to do, so he bought time. "If you didn't mean to keep your word, why did you bother drawing accurate maps?"

"Truth is, I drew 'em for meself, so's I wouldn't forget me way back here one day. The prison camp commander wound up with 'em, and it was me stay in your fine detention facility that prompted me to go to him, explain what they were, and offer the trade. I'd a give up me dear silver-haired mother to get outa that hole."

"I've heard that about you."

O'Kelly frowned. "Now Johnnie, you're in no position to be sassin me. The slightest little annoyance might cause me to flinch and accidently blow a hole right through you. Understand?"

"I do. But I don't understand how you got here. I'd wager it wasn't on a horse."

"You've got that right, Johnnie. Once I made me way to Washington – no small feat, I might add, what with changin uniforms an makin up stories at the drop of a hat – it was easy to disappear in the crowd. I simply rolled drunks and whores until I had a stake and made me way to Denver by coach and train, layin over when there was no ride to be had. I'd recommend the train, Johnnie, if you're ever travelin up north where they're still runnin." O'Kelly grinned and went on. "Now, you tell *me* a secret. How many men have you got left?"

"None. The handful still living have headed home to Texas. You started quite a ruckus back there." Drake thought it unlikely that O'Kelly had stuck around to watch the fight, considering the job Gage and the Gatling gun had done on his rifle perch.

"Well, now, we'll have to wait'n see if you're tellin the truth about your boys, but the ruckus was for a good cause. I was aimin at that miserable son-of-a-bitch of an Apache, the one the pepper-bellies think can't be killed, that they call *el Milagro*. He was fond of puttin me on a leash an lettin the young savages play with me like some dog. Would you be so kind as to tell me if I got the bastard?"

Drake nodded toward the Spencer. "When a man opens up with a carbine from that range, he's not particular what he hits. I take that personally, O'Kelly."

O'Kelly wagged the carbine at Drake. "I've spoken to you about your disrespectful tone, laddybuck. If I were you, I'd be careful."

"And if I were you," Drake replied, "I wouldn't bother packing that stuff down the mountain."

"Oh, I believe I'll go to the trouble, Johnnie. You see, I done twenty years in this man's army, an for what? I got no qualms about takin it. I was all for takin it on the way to Fort Craig, but some of the boys were fearful the rumors weren't true, an if we broke the seal to find out, there'd be hell to pay. In fact, we were havin one helluva row about it when the greasers jumped us. But they didn't kill me, nor the Injuns, nor you lot. I figger if there's anybody charmed, it's me, an not that smelly savage. Nobody's gonna stop me." He leveled the carbine. "And I'm afraid, Johnnie, that includes you."

Drake knew there was no more time to buy. "Do you have a knife?"

O'Kelly tilted his head and grinned. "Why, you know, I was plannin to shoot you, Johnnie, but a knife ain't a bad idea, on account of you might have some friends back down the trail. But only if that's what you'd prefer."

"Cut into one of those bars, and you'll see why it's not worth hauling."

He scowled. "What're you sayin'?"

"I'm saying they sent you out to get killed guarding a shipment of lead. Look at the corner of that bar on top."

O'Kelly looked, and saw the gray dent. He unsheathed a skinning knife as he knelt beside the pile, his breath quickening. Pointing the Spencer at Drake with an unsteady left hand, he cut an eighth-inch gouge into the edge of the ingot, clearly revealing the lead beneath the thin layer of gold.

"No," he said, unable to accept the truth. "Mother of Christ! No!"

Milagro's leap started fifteen feet away, in the boulders to O'Kelly's right. His foot landed on O'Kelly's forearm, jarring the Spencer loose as he grabbed O'Kelly by the shirt and threw him into the rock wall near the cave. Drake dove for his revolvers, shucking one free of its holster as the Apache shoved O'Kelly against the granite, a knife at his throat.

Drake thumbed back the hammer on the Colt as he rose to one knee. "No," he said. "*Alto!*"

Milagro remained motionless, his hot eyes fixed on O'Kelly's. "I will kill him, unless you kill me," he said, in Spanish.

O'Kelly's breath came in rapid bursts. "Christ, Johnnie, I

wasn't goin to harm you! I was only havin' some fun." He spoke in a raspy whisper, as if to keep the Apache from over-hearing. "But this heathen won't rest 'til every white man in the territory's dead. For the love of God, shoot the son-of-a-bitch!"

"Good idea," Drake said, and pulled the trigger. Milagro released O'Kelly and let him slide down the wall to a sitting position, eyes wide and mouth agape. His lips moved, but no sound emerged as he slumped over and died.

Drake stood up, then lowered the Colt as he walked through the smoke toward the Apache. "He was the one shooting from the rocks," he said, in Spanish.

"I heard," Milagro replied, in English. "I know the words. It is better if the bluecoats don't know I understand them when they speak."

Drake nodded. "I could kill you right now. Why did you risk your life for me?"

Milagro spread his arms. "Maybe there are twenty warriors with rifles aimed at you. What do I risk?"

Drake knew there weren't any warriors around. He felt he understood the Apache, and the Apache understood him.

"I have no gold to trade," Milagro said. "I give you your life for the gun that keeps shooting."

Drake shook his head. "I can't do that."

"I will kill many bluecoats. It will be good for the gray-coats."

"The bluecoats have defeated us, and they will defeat you. They have many men and guns, and real gold to buy what-ever they need. The young bluecoat officer was going to ask you to surrender and save your people's lives."

Milagro scoffed at the notion. "My people will not live at

Bosque Redondo, begging for scraps and stealing blankets from the Navaho to keep from freezing. If the bluecoats want peace with me, why will they not leave Apache land to the Apache?"

"They don't want peace, they want this land. And they will take it for the same reason the Apache take blankets from the Navahos, and horses and cattle from the white settlers. They want it, and they're strong enough to take it. You can't imagine how many men and guns they can send against you. You won't stop them with a hundred of those guns that keep shooting. They'll kill every one of you if you keep fighting."

Sgt. Gage could hear the voices, but the old man couldn't quite make out the conversation. Stepping into the clearing, he glimpsed the menacing visage of an angry Apache warrior with a knife in his hand, glaring at his captain. He dropped to one knee and brought up his Enfield.

Drake shouted, "No!" but the word was lost in the roar of the gunshot.

They found Milagro's horse hidden and tied not far from Drake's. Sgt. Cage couldn't understand why a healthy horse had to be killed, or why a perfectly good Henry rifle needed to be entombed with its owner in the cave, but the captain insisted, so that was what they did. At the base of the mountain they felled enough pinion pines to make a good sized fire under and around the Gatling gun and the remaining ammunition. When the gun was fully engulfed and the cartridges were beginning to explode, Drake turned away and walked to his waiting troopers, where a downcast Sgt. Gage stood holding both their horses.

Taking the reins of Lt. Tyler's horse, Drake wearily hoisted himself into the saddle. "Sam," he said, "let's go home."

EPILOGUE

That evening Lt. William Tyler died in an ambulance en route to Fort Craig, clutching a small photograph of his wife. A well worn, standard issue Confederate cavalry officer's saber was at his side. Based on Lt. Tyler's report to the leader of the patrol that found him, the commanding officer at Fort Craig declined to pursue the departing rebels.

Shortly after dawn on August 9th that year, a day's march east of Fort Craig, five Apache warriors armed with knives and war clubs attacked a bivouacked infantry company. They killed eleven soldiers and wounded four others before the last brave was shot. Five days later the remnants of Milagro's band came in to the fort and surrendered and were taken to Bosque Redondo.

Harlan Drake returned to San Antonio to find his herd gone. Any cattle not run off by the Comanche had long since been commandeered by the Confederacy. He acquired twenty cows and a longhorn bull and began again. In the spring of 1866 he married Catherine Ann Stuart, the thirty-year-old widow of his second lieutenant. He raised her two daughters as his own, and on June 5th, 1867, Catherine gave birth to their only child. Although the boy's given name was William, his father sometimes called him Miracle Boy.

The End

Kenneth Mark Hoover –

Kenneth Mark Hoover has sold over fifty short stories and articles. His fiction has appeared in magazines such as *Fantastic Stories, Strange Horizons, Challenging Destiny, Three Crow Press* and the new science fiction anthology *Destination: Future*. His first novel, *Fevreblau*, was published by Five Star Press in 2005. His story "Haxan," set in the same world as "White Hawk," appeared in Beneath Ceaseless Skies #13. Mr. Hoover currently lives in Dallas, TX.

WHITE HAWK

Kenneth Mark Hoover

I walked between the bodies. Everyone was dead. Horses, dogs, men.

The smoke from the burning wagons towered like black pillars against the blue, unwinking sky. Canvas from the canopy ribs snapped and tore in flaming shreds. Sometimes the wind moaned through the broken wheels like a ghost trying to find his way home.

There were a lot of ghosts here.

Jake leaned forward in his saddle. "I don't know why we live here, Marshal Marwood. The desert . . . it kills people."

A young girl lay at my feet. Her green dress was torn. "The desert didn't do this, Jake."

"Apache? Savage enough. And they didn't just count coup."

I studied the arrow in the back of a man. He was face down, holding the girl. He had tried to protect her with his last breath. Her father, maybe, or brother.

I put my boot against him, took hold of the shaft and pulled it free. "Look at this point, Jake, and the fletching. That's not Apache."

"Navajo." He tossed the arrow away. "That's not like them. They're mostly peaceful folk."

"Someone made them mad." I took the reins from Jake and swung into my saddle. "We'd better find out why."

"But, Mr. Marwood, we're riding to Las Cruces to pick up a prisoner. Sheriff White is waiting with transfer papers."

"Henry White can hold that man a while longer. If renegades jumped the reservation, they might hit Haxan next. They're headed in the right direction. We can't let that happen."

I had come a long way through time and wind and dust to make sure something like that never happened. Either to the town, or her.

We followed the unshod pony tracks. It was hard to judge on the hard earth, but it looked like twenty or thirty horses in the war party. "A good sized group, Jake, moving fast."

"Lucky thing we were skirting Crooked Mesa to the east or we'd have never found them." He turned round in his saddle. "Six wagons. And they didn't have time to circle up and defend themselves."

I pointed to a hillock a hundred yards away. "Looks like the war party came over that rise. Let's ride that way." Jake pulled his rifle from his boot. The desert was quiet around us. We were holding our breaths, too.

I was thinking about the dead girl. Her hair was long and black. Just like Magra's.

"My stars, can you imagine what it was like?" Jake whispered. "Thirty men on war ponies screaming out of the sun. It's enough to freeze your blood."

"That's enough, Jake."

"Yes, sir."

We topped the rise. "Oh, no . . . ."

A cabin a quarter mile below was wreathed in flames. There were more people on the ground. All the livestock were dead.

All men are born of blood. We die that way, too.

It is the blood of our family and friends that ties us together. Makes us human. Gives us enemies.

I cannot remember how long I have traveled or from what depths I arose. I only know I am here now, brought to stand against that which must be overcome. As all my people are.

"I telegraphed Fort Providence before the lines were cut. A war party of fifty jumped the reservation two days ago and another one, a smaller one, yesterday. Two more this morning. Something's got them stirred up."

Mayor Frank Polgar and Doc Toland were standing in my office looking nervous and unsure. Jake was oiling his Winchester.

Mayor Polgar had thinning red hair and watery blue eyes. His face was drawn and yellow in the desert morning light streaming through the open window. "Who's in command there?"

"Colonel Chapman. I've dealt with him. He's competent. They've got a troop trying to run this first war party, the big one, along the El Camino Real. No luck so far."

"What do you think we should do, Marshal Marwood?"

"People are safe if they remain in town. It looks like this southern party is hitting up and down the territory, restricting their terror to Sangre County. But they're by-passing towns like Haxan and Glaze."

"Are these random attacks, John?" That was Doc Toland, a grizzled man in a black frock with dusty cuffs. I remembered the night Ben Tack gunned me down and Doc Toland running across the plaza toward me.

"No, Doc, more like they're looking for something. Or someone."

The two men exchanged swift glances. Polgar squinted in disbelief. "Say again, Marshal?"

I turned to the yellowed map of Sangre County framed behind my desk. "Here's where they hit that wagon train we found. This was the cabin on a little farm where a creek hits the rise. And an hour ago I got a report of a whiskey drummer who had his mule train attacked before sundown. It's scattered all over the county. Back and forth along this line between Crooked Mesa and Coldwater."

"That's a lot of territory, Marshal."

"The attacks are concentrated there. That first party, well, if you ask me it's a feint to give this second party time to attack in force."

"But, if they're raiding up and down –"

"This isn't a raiding party, Mayor. Jake and I saw those wagons. They were fired and broken, but they weren't ransacked. Nothing was stolen, except for maybe guns and ammunition, which you would expect. Same on the farm. Everybody was just . . . dead."

"Scalped?"

"They were dead. Let's leave it at that."

Jake put his Winchester down and loaded Magra's old shotgun, clicked the breech shut. He handed it to me. "I'm ready, Mr. Marwood."

Polgar gaped. "Where are you going?" He and Doc Toland

followed us out of the office and onto Front Street. "You have to stay and protect the town, Marshal. Both you and your deputy."

"No, we don't, Mayor. I told you these renegades are skirting big settlements. If they're roaming the countryside then that's where we need to be. Maybe we can run them down and learn what this is about."

"This is an Army problem. Let them handle it."

"And I'm a U.S. Marshal, which makes it federal business. Anyway, Fort Providence is chasing that group up north. This smaller war party is our problem. Keep everyone inside and no one will get hurt." I mounted my blue roan and he kicked a little. He was always able to smell blood coming.

"I mean it, Frank. I don't want any posses forming up without my knowledge. I won't stand for it. Doc, you get the word out, too."

Doc waved his understanding. Polgar had his hand on the bridle of my horse. "You're taking an awful risk, John."

"I'll handle this problem my way, Frank."

"How?"

"I'm headed for Magra Snowberry's place. She's part Navajo and they've always trusted her. Maybe she has some idea what this is about."

Jake and I kicked for the old Shiner Larsen place. As we rode through town several shopkeepers called from their doorways for us to stay. The plaza was empty. People were scared and I couldn't blame them. We followed the road out and cut across country to save time.

Magra's place – everyone called it the Shiner Larsen place after her dead father – was on a small rise where Gila Creek turned through a field of boulders. Jake and I were skirting the last big boulder when we reined our horses hard enough to cause them to stumble and snort.

"My . . . stars," Jake whispered in awe.

Magra's little cabin was surrounded by Navajo braves mounted on sleek, painted ponies. There must have been a hundred or more and they were wearing war paint.

"Ride easy, Jake," I said. "Keep your hands in sight or we'll both end up as a smear spot on the desert floor."

"You think they're holding Miss Magra hostage?"

"I don't know. Come on."

We rode slow. Their hard faces watched us come. We pulled short ten yards away.

"Now what?" Jake wondered.

"Let them make the first move."

The door to Magra's cabin opened and a tall Navajo wearing breechclout, moccasins and an imposing war headdress came out. His face was marked by the New Mexican desert and wind, his shoulders burned red from the blistering sun. He had a single white feather tied around his neck. Magra emerged after him, unharmed. She wore buckskin instead of her usual calico, perhaps as a concession to her people. Even her hair was tied back Indian fashion.

Addressing the war chief standing at her side, she pointed at me.

"That's him," she said. "The man known as Long Blood."

Thermopylae. Masada. Agincourt.

And now Haxan, New Mexico.

We have many different names, we who come. Some are unpronounceable and even we don't know them all. I don't think we're supposed to because it would be too overwhelming. But we all have names and some are taller than others.

We go where we are needed.

I have a name. Lots of them. And when I am called I stand against that which must be faced. I have done it since the beginning of time.

You see, there is a thing inside me, coiled in wintry sleep. Rarely does it awake. But when it does I let it have full voice.

It's who I am. It's my Name.

"I am White Hawk," the war chief said.

I had a name in his tongue, too, but he probably wouldn't believe it. "My name is John Marwood. I'm a U.S. Marshal for this territory. This is my deputy, Jake Strop."

"My people know you as Long Blood. I will call you that. We will talk between us, Long Blood. I have much to say and I will listen to you as well."

"I think that's a fine idea, White Hawk."

"We will speak inside Magra's lodge. She is a daughter of our nation. Her words and her heart are made straight."

"I think so, too."

"We will sit at table as White Men do so you will know my words have serious meaning."

"I appreciate that, White Hawk." It was a big concession on his behalf and I wondered why he was making it. "Jake, stay out here. White Hawk's men won't hurt you. Magra . . . ."

She smiled at me. It always made me feel good when she smiled. "I'm all right, John. I'll stay with Jake. Go inside and listen to what White Hawk has to say. I . . . I hope you can help him."

I nodded and followed the other man inside. We sat across the table, hands crossed before us. We studied each other for several moments before he began to speak in slow, measured words.

"The roof of Magra's lodge is open to the sky." He meant he didn't want there to be any half-truths between us.

"It's a good place for men to talk," I agreed.

"I have killed many Whites these past days."

"It has to stop, White Hawk."

"I cannot stop, Long Blood." His sadness sounded genuine. "I must keep killing until I find that which we have lost."

"What did you lose?"

But I was pushing him too hard. His pride and his culture would not allow him to be so direct. "My great-grandfather, Crooked Tent, told me stories of how it was before the Whites came. He taught me our people believe all things are living in this world, so we should not be surprised there are other men who also live. But over the years I have learned the White doesn't believe all things live. To him, all things are dead. Even other men who are living are still dead in their eyes. This makes their hearts hard and they have no reverence for those who are truly dead. I admit this saddens me as a human being."

White Hawk took a deep breath and stared at the table. He was moved by his own words. "We have allowed our Nation to be put on land that is not ours. By doing this we have let the hearts of our fathers to be cut." He raised his face. Now his eyes found mine. "But it is not my hand that broke the treaty. I am White Hawk. I speak straight."

"I know you do, White Hawk." His talk about reverence for those who are dead had me thinking. "Listen. Did something happen with your burial grounds?"

He gave a solemn nod but didn't speak further. Now I understood why he was so reticent, why it was such a battle for him to reveal what was bothering him. It wasn't the topic itself, but the cultural embarrassment mixed with anger.

"We are in Magra's house," I reminded him, "a place of friendship between men who can trust one another. Like you said, her roof is open to the sky. Tell me what happened, White Hawk. Magra seems to think I can help."

The stoic man appeared to resolve some internal conflict. He started by pushing the words out, but then they came more easily.

"You know something of our medicine, Long Blood. Our burial grounds are sacred. Last week men dug holes in the earth and put the bodies of our dead in them. They said their own spirit words from the book they lean upon. Then they went away after violating the quiet medicine of that place."

That was bad enough, but there was more. "When the moon was orange a Navajo maiden died of sleep fever. Her name was Morning Star. Her passing cut the heart from my body forever and made me lose my memory." He made a motion with his hands to signify the pain he felt. "She was brought to the burial grounds in the tradition of my people so her body could cross into the spirit world. But when those men came she was not put in the ground with the others they defiled. Morning Star was stolen."

I couldn't believe what I was hearing. All too often settlers moving through the territory who didn't know any better precipitated cultural clashes with the various Indian tribes. But I had never heard of anything like this. No wonder the entire Navajo nation was up in arms.

"Who did this, White Hawk?"

Kenneth Mark Hoover

"One of the Great Wheels that destroy the ground and make the buffalo that remain stampede before them."

The wagon trains moving through the El Camino Real. "Why did they steal Morning Star's body?"

"She was beautiful even in death. She was dressed in white, and wore beads, and her hair was braided in the fashion of our dead. Too, it is not unknown for men of your race to take totems and fetishes from our burial grounds and sell them to people in the East. They put them in their own lodges and make themselves feel superior to people whose shoulders are burned red from the desert sun."

He let out a long, slow breath. I thought he was relieved, now that he had unburdened himself. "While riding, the power of my memory returned. I remembered Magra. And how there was a man of blood and violence who cared for her. I spoke words with Magra. She told me a man known to love a half-white Navajo girl was someone I could trust."

"I hope so."

"That is my story, Marshal Who is Long Blood." His voice was deep and measured . . . and full of conviction. "They stole Morning Star's body. Now I kill Whites. And I will keep killing until her body is returned to my people."

I rode with White Hawk for five days through the El Camino Real. I never knew there were so many people on the move. We came upon camps and river sites and way stations searching for a wagon train that had passed through Indian burial grounds when the moon was orange.

We had a fair idea where the train might be found. After all, they can only make so many miles a day. Given the relation of the burial grounds, and the fact wagons stick to well-marked trails, it should have been easy.

But there was a lot of territory to cover.

The Navajo nation was standing down for the moment. It hadn't been an easy armistice to arrange. White Hawk said if I helped find Morning Star before the next moon he would call off the slaughter. That didn't leave me much time. Meanwhile, the Army sharpened their sabers and the Navajo braves sang their death songs.

One thing stood in our favor. The entire countryside was talking about it, which helped and hindered our search. Most people were supportive, understanding White Hawk's shame, while others were downright hostile. It felt like we were riding through a powder keg and every day the fuse sputtered closer.

With two days remaining before the new moon we found the wagon train we were looking for twenty miles south of Santa Fe. There were four wagons in the train. One had broken its whiffletree and they had stopped to carve a new one. If the wagon hadn't broken down we would have missed them by two hours.

Like I said, we go where we're sent. But sometimes it seemed those who send us were also looking out for us. I didn't really believe it, mind you. But it was nice to think it could be true when you have to stand against that which must be faced.

It was going on toward evening. The sky in the west was a cauldron of fire.

The people we were looking for had a big central campfire going with the wagons parked around it. White Hawk and I let the horses browse while we walked out of the gathering dark.

I warned White Hawk to let me do the talking. His non-commital grunt didn't make me optimistic. His eyes glared with hate.

"Hello in the camp," I called.

I heard the distinct click of a gun. I put an arm cross White Hawk's chest to hold him up. I think he would have kept on walking right into the gunfire. He was that angry.

"Who is it?" Gruff voice. Challenging. And a little frightened.

"My name is John T. Marwood. I'm a federal officer." I opened my grey duster so he could see the glint of my badge. "I'm a United States Marshal. Mind if we share your fire?"

"Who is with you, Marshal?"

"You know his name."

"Let me hear him say it," the voice demanded.

"I am White Hawk. I come for the woman you stole."

"Let them in, Paul." This second voice was measured with a fair hint of education behind it. "We can't keep running."

"Come easy, both of you."

We walked between two wagons and into the shifting camp light. Two men stood beside the main fire. One held a double-barreled shotgun with the hammers pulled back. He had a round bearded face and heavy shoulders. His partner was lean and clean-shaven with a wide-brimmed hat, fancy striped waistcoat and silver watch chain.

There were a dozen other people, too, keeping to the relative safety of the wagons. Families holding their grubby children, and all with desperation burning in their eyes.

Everyone was staring but they weren't fixed on me. It was likely they had never seen an Indian up close. All they knew were stories from penny dreadfuls and tall tales heard around a drunken camp fire.

The lean man broke the silence once we had taken measure. "Marshal, my name is Dr. Robert Carver Graves. This is Mr. Paul Hickle. I hired him for protection while traveling out West. Put your gun down, Paul, it's okay. Marshal, I want you to know we never meant any harm, but –"

"Where is she, Graves?"

"In that wagon yonder. Wrapped in canvas and packed in a barrel of salt and charcoal."

White Hawk started beside me. "I want to see," he told me. I nodded for him to go ahead. The people beside the wagon ran aside to clear the way. He crawled into the wagon and disappeared.

I turned to face Graves. "What for?"

"What? Oh, so the body will be preserved, Marshal. We're going to ship it East by rail. But once word got out we thought it prudent to keep it until the brush fire burned itself out. If you get my meaning." Graves tried a knowing smile on me. When I didn't respond he wiped it off quick.

Paul Hickle chimed in. "This here is an important man, Marshal. You would do a better to treat Professor Graves with respect."

"Is that why he hides dead Indian maidens in freight wagons and hires a melon head like you to protect him?"

Hickle's face closed down. His hand tightened on the stock of the gun. "There's no call for that talk, Marshal. We ain't done nothing bad wrong. We gave those bodies a Christian burial. Only a godless savage would leave them to rot out in the sun like that."

"Gentlemen, please." Graves glanced at the wagon in question and cleared his throat. "Look, Marshal, let me explain. I'm a natural history curator for the Smithsonian Institution and a founding member of the Megatherium Club. Though that guild disbanded in 1866 many of us continue to work for the museum. I collect and classify anthropological specimens. My particular expertise is primitive cultures, documenting them as they become extinct. From a scientific point of view we must have a record of these cultures that are disappearing from the West as they are supplanted by a superior one. Therefore, you can realize –"

"You can stop now."

"What's that, Marshal?"

"Talking. You can stop."

"Why, Marshal, I'm just trying to explain –"

"I said shut up."

"You can't talk to Professor Graves that way," Hickle bristled.

I met his eyes. "That's where you're wrong."

One of the women screamed. White Hawk walked from the wagon with a long canvas-wrapped body doubled in his arms.

"Where does he think he's going?" Graves blustered. "That's a very valuable artifact!"

White Hawk approached me. His face was stone. "I will need fire."

"I understand." I had spent enough time with this man to know what was going on inside him. I motioned to the settlers standing around and gawking. "Start gathering wood for a bonfire."

Graves rushed forward, waving his hands. "Wait one blessed minute. You can't order these people around. I'm in charge of this expedition."

The men and women, for their part, were uncertain. "Do what I told you," I told them. They looked at me and Graves and started stacking fresh wood in the clearing.

Graves pushed through the working throng and stood in front of me. "I protest this outrage to the highest degree, Marshal. I'll telegraph Washington and have your badge pulled. I am trying to preserve the memory of this declining culture. How can I make you understand that?"

"Graves, if you say one more word I'm going to shoot you."

He opened his mouth to protest and found himself staring down the iron barrel of my Colt Dragoon. Sweat glistened on his wide forehead.

"Easy, Marshal," Hickle growled. "I've got this shotgun trained on your back."

"Don't be a fool, Hickle. You kill me and you, and all these other people, will never see the sun rise."

"Don't bluff me, Marshal. I'm the one holding the shot-gun."

"Look around you, Hickle."

"All I see is you about to be cut in two squirming halves."

"No, melon head, around you. Through those wagons over yonder. And to my right. Now do you see what I'm talking about?"

"Oh, my God . . . ."

The others looked too. They screamed and fell over themselves, dropping firewood and crowding like sheep in the center of the wagon ring.

There were hundreds of Navajo braves dressed in war paint and standing in the dark. They were armed. They drew closer. The light from the campfire played over their features and limbs.

"Put your shotgun down, Hickle," I told him. "And do it slow. That's right." Maybe he was smart after all. "Now, professor, or whatever you want to call yourself, back up against that wagon there. The rest of you settlers, keep stacking that firewood. Go on, do as I say. These braves won't hurt you."

With reluctance and then renewed energy the Whites gathered the remaining firewood, carried it to the clearing. All the while White Hawk stood with Morning Star cradled in his arms.

While they were getting the bonfire prepared I walked over to the wagon White Hawk had searched. Inside were crates and barrels and hundreds of glass bottles. More specimens. I pulled one of the men aside helping build the bonfire.

"Whose wagon is this?"

"It belongs to Dr. Graves. We met him in St. Louis and he asked if he and his bodyguard could come along. We thought there would be safety in numbers. We never knew anything like this was going to happen. We thought we were doing right burying those exposed bodies, Marshal. That part is true, we never meant harm. But then we started hearing stories about how the Indians were on the warpath because a burial site had been raided. We knew we were responsible and wanted to say it. But Professor Graves, he said the furor would die down if we laid low long enough. Hickle backed him up with his shotgun. We sure didn't mean to cause trouble."

"What's your name, mister?"

"Joyce. Caspar Joyce."

"Where are you headed, Mr. Joyce?"

"Wyoming." He watched the braves and swallowed audibly. "I have a wife and two small children, Marshal. I hope we get out of this with a whole skin."

"You're not going to be hurt. These people will go home once they finish what they have to do."

"Maybe so." He looked at me. "Marshal, there's something I don't understand."

"What's that?"

"Well, sir, doesn't this land belong to whoever can hold it?"

It was a dark night. All the world was dark, maybe. I guess it's always that way, though.

"I'm not sure I understand you, Mr. Joyce."

"The Indians had this land for a long time. Now it belongs to us. Our people. One day, someone will push us off. That's how life works, Marshal. May not be fair, but no one ever said life was fair."

"Better get back to work, Mr. Joyce. They're almost done."

"Yes, sir." He left me and I joined White Hawk.

"No one is going to stop you," I told him low. Graves was still standing by himself but I was keeping an eye on him.

"I want to thank you, Long Blood," White Hawk said. He had been holding Morning Star all this time and showed no sign of fatigue. "And Morning Star's spirit wishes to thank you, too. Now she will cross to the other side and have a guide to make sure she won't get lost. She will rest in the morning sky, thanks to you."

"Goodbye, White Hawk."

"Goodbye, Long Blood. Magra was right. You are a man who can also be a brother."

Everyone drew back leaving White Hawk all alone. He laid Morning Star on the pyre and raised his face to the starry heavens. He lifted his hands and began to sing. Tears fell from his eyes into his open mouth.

When he finished singing he took a flaming brand from the smaller campfire and lighted the dry wood. It caught easily. He stepped into the smoke and flame and stretched out to sleep beside Morning Star. The flames leaped higher, whorling around their bodies like a tornado. They burned for a long time.

When it was finished the remaining Navajo braves melted into the night. When the fire died down the sky to the east was tinged with pink.

There wasn't much left of the pyre but I picked up a smoldering brand and walked toward the far wagon.

Graves threw himself at me. "No, you can't! I won't let you!"

Hickle grabbed the older man's shirt and pulled him back. "Dr. Graves, those Indians are still out there. We have no choice. We have to do it."

"Out of the way, Graves." I pushed him aside and pitched the lighted brand into the rear of the wagon. There must have been loose straw or something back there because it caught fast.

The other settlers were packing their wagons and getting ready to pull out in the grey morning. Hickle wrestled with Graves until the latter suddenly lost any fight he had left. Graves watched his specimens and artifacts go up in smoke and flame.

He turned on me, snarling. "Does it give you satisfaction, Marshal?"

"As a matter of fact, Dr. Graves, it doesn't. But I don't expect you to understand that."

I put my back to him and walked out of the wagon ring to find my horse.

"You must realize you haven't changed a thing," Graves shouted. His voice sounded thin in the wide open desert. "The West will die and their culture will die and nothing you or I or anyone can do will ever change that. Marshal! All you did was destroy the memory and record of that change. All you did was destroy yourself!"

A half hour later I caught my horse and rode along the spine of a hogback. Half a mile away three wagons creaked toward the West. A tiny dot followed behind on foot. I watched them disappear in the desert haze.

Magra. She had long hair tied back Indian fashion and it always smelled clean and crisp. I wanted to see her.

I turned my horse toward a bright star that was rising with the morning and rode straight into it.

The End

Larry Payne –

Larry Payne grew up in East Chicago, Indiana, and now resides in Chandler, Arizona with his wife, Susan, and their two cats, Molly and Emily.

He is a US Navy veteran where he served as a Hospital Corpsman. He is currently employed at Banner Heart Hospital in Mesa, AZ, as a Cardiac Monitor Technician.

Besides his western fiction short stories that have appeared on Frontier Tales, he has written short stories of crime fiction and science fiction.

The release date of his western fiction novella, *Ride the Savage Land*, by Wild Child Publishing, is yet to be determined.

Larry's e-mail address is ecwalum@yahoo.com.

Check out his web site at www.larrypayne.jimdo.com and his blog at http://larrypayneauthor.blogspot.com

His tweet address is @LarryPayne2.

AND HELL CAME WITH HIM

Larry Payne

Lightning streaked the darkened sky above the solemn group around the grave. The Preacher, standing at the head of the grave, read passages from his worn Bible as four men, dressed in black suits, grasped the ends of the two ropes stretched under both ends of the wooden coffin. Slowly, they moved the coffin over the open grave and began to lower it.

A woman's white-gloved hand appeared from the coffin, sliding the lid to the side. She reached out to the group above.

"WIL, NO. DON'T LET ME GO."

Wil Sunday sat upright in his bed. With a chill running over his sweat soaked body, he looked around the moonlit bedroom. The recurring nightmare was a frequent part of his nights since he buried his beloved wife, Cassie.

He swung his legs over the side of the bed and sat staring at the floor. Finally rising, he lifted his pants from the chair next to the bed and stepped into them. Running his fingers through his hair, he walked from the bedroom to the front door.

The cool night breeze greeted him as he walked out and sat down on the edge of the porch, looking up at the full moon amid the dark blanket of twinkling stars. His big, brown dog, Buck, who had followed him out the door, lay down next to him, resting his head in Wil's lap. Wil looked around the yard, and the events of that tragic day flooded back to him.

Wil was repairing a harness in the barn when the three gunmen rode up to the house. Buck's barking brought him out of the barn. Seeing the three riders, he went to the front of the house.

"Howdy," said the rider closest to Wil. The first to speak, Wil figured this was the leader.

Wil walked up beside Buck, who was growling at the new arrivals, and patted him on the neck to calm him down. He looked at each of the three riders in turn, all hardcases.

"Your dog's a mite unfriendly," added the gray-haired rider.

"He doesn't like strangers. What can I do for you fellas?"

Just then, Cassie walked out of the house onto the porch. Her appearance got the attention of the four outlaws.

"I think you and your missus can do quite a lot for us."

Suddenly, Wil wished he hadn't left his rifle in the house. With a slight nod of his head, he motioned Cassie back into the house.

"I've got work to do, so I'd be obliged if you'd water your horses and be on your way."

"Yeah, so do we," said the outlaw, drawing his Colt as his two companions dismounted.

Wil dove as the outlaw fired, feeling an intense pain in his side. Despite the burning pain, he tried to get up. The outlaw fired a second time, hitting Wil in the shoulder, knocking him to the ground again.

The outlaw stepped down from his horse, looking at the still form of Wil Sunday. He thumbed the spent shells from his Colt and replaced them from his gunbelt. He dropped the Colt back into its holster, turned and followed his men into the house.

Wil opened his eyes as the gunman disappeared into the house. Cassie's screams were the last thing he heard before succumbing to the darkness.

Buck licked Wil's face, interrupting his thoughts, bringing him back. He scratched Buck behind the ears.

"I guess it's just you and me now, boy."

Wil stood up, walked down the two steps of the porch and went toward the barn. Stopping at the barn door, he lit the lantern with the matches he kept on the shelf beside it. Taking the lantern to the ladder at the far side of the barn, he climbed to the loft.

Setting the lantern on the floor, he grabbed a pitchfork and began moving hay from a corner of the loft. Uncovering a trunk, he dragged it clear of the hay and removed a wooden peg from the hasp.

Opening the trunk lid, Wil lifted a small tarp covering the contents of the trunk. A low crowned, flat brimmed hat was the first thing he removed from the trunk. Laying it on the open trunk lid, he pulled out an empty holster and gunbelt and laid it next to the hat.

Next, he unwrapped a well-oiled, sightless Colt from an oilskin and slid it into the holster. He removed a Henry rifle lying across a stack of clothes and leaned it against the side of the trunk.

A Bowie knife came next. Removing it from the scabbard, he lightly ran his thumb along the edge of the blade testing its sharpness. Satisfied, he slid the broad blade back into the leather scabbard, laying it on the trunk lid.

He lifted the clothes to uncover two boxes of shells each for the Colt and the Henry rifle. Repacking the trunk, he closed the lid and slipped the wood peg back through the hasp.

Wil took the end of a coiled rope and strung it through a pulley above the edge of the loft. Dragging the trunk to the edge of the loft, he tied the other end of the rope to a leather handle on one end of the trunk and gently lowered it to the floor of the barn.

Buck was waiting for him when he stepped off the bottom rung of the ladder. He untied the rope and after a short struggle, maneuvered the trunk onto his back.

Carrying it into the house, he lowered the trunk to the bedroom floor. Reopening the trunk, he laid the contents on the bed. Picking up the gunbelt, he buckled it around his waist, thonging the holster to his left thigh. He lifted the Colt and settled it gently back in the holster.

Wil caught his reflection in the full-length mirror that stood in the corner. Turning toward it, he looked at his reflection for a moment, suddenly drawing his Colt. Wil looked at the Colt, then down at Buck who was watching curiously.

"We've got a lot of work to do."

Wil practiced tirelessly day after day. When the shell boxes were empty, he bought more. The days turned into weeks, until finally, the speed came back. The accuracy followed close behind, but he had to be sure.

One morning he brought Miguel Saldano, his farmhand,

to the field where he practiced, handing Miguel a tin can.

"Miguel, walk about twenty paces and hold that can out."

"Señor?" said Miguel, an alarmed look spreading across his face.

"Trust me, Miguel." Hesitantly, Miguel marched twenty paces and turned around.

"Hold the can out," said Wil, holding his arm at shoulder level. Miguel raised his arm.

"Drop the can whenever you're ready."

After a moment, Miguel released the can. At the first sign of movement, Wil became a blur of motion, drawing his Colt, shooting the can at waist level.

Wil asked Miguel to retrieve the can, this time holding it waist high. Again, Wil shot the can before it touched the ground.

"Madre de Dios," said Miguel, crossing himself. "I did not know you could shoot like that, Señor."

Wil walked toward Miguel as he reloaded his Colt and dropped it back into its holster.

"You go after Señora Cassie's killers? You wish Miguel to go with you?"

Wil put his arm around Miguel's shoulders as they walked toward the house.

"Miguel, I want you and Maria to run the farm while I'm gone."

Miguel stopped and looked at Wil.

"Me, Señor?"

Wil smiled at Miguel.

"You've been with me from the start, Miguel. You can run this farm as good as I can. I'll make all the arrangements to make sure you get all the help you'll need."

"I will do my best, Señor Wil."

Wil left Miguel in the yard and went into the house. In the bedroom, Wil removed the clothes from the trunk, putting on the Levis and the blue cotton shirt. He put on a black leather vest over the shirt. After stomping into his boots, Wil put the leather scabbard and the Bowie knife on his gunbelt and rebuckled the Colt around his waist, rethonging the holster to his left thigh. Finally, he settled the black hat on his head.

Grabbing the Henry rifle from a corner by the dresser, he walked from the bedroom to the kitchen where Miguel and Maria waited.

"Move your things into the house," said Wil.

Maria threw her arms around Wil's neck and gave him a hug.

"Thank you, Señor Wil. I will pray that you find the men that did this thing. Come back safe to us."

Wil hugged Maria for a moment and then shook Miguel's hand.

"I'm taking Cassie's Palomino. Buck is going with me too."

"Si, Señor," said Miguel, "She is a good horse and Buck will watch out for you."

Wil went to the barn and saddled the golden Palomino that was Cassie's pride and joy. She had not been ridden since Cassie's death. Throwing his saddlebags behind the saddle, he put the Henry rifle in the saddle boot.

Walking the horse outside, he stepped into the saddle. He could feel the anticipation of the powerful horse. She hadn't run in a long time. He waved at Miguel and Maria standing on the porch as he rode out of the yard.

"Vaya con Dios, Señor," whispered Miguel.

Wil Sunday rode into Beecher a little past noon. His unusual dress attracted attention as he dismounted in front of the bank. Withdrawing one thousand dollars from his account, he asked to see bank president, Hiram Willis.

"I want to authorize Miguel Saldano to make any withdrawals or deposits as needed on my account."

After a mild objection, Hiram Willis drew up the paperwork for Wil to sign. Next, he made stops at the general store and hardware store before dismounting in front of the sheriff's office.

"I wondered when you were going to get around to this," said Sheriff Logan Shepherd, eyeing the thronged-down Colt when Wil walked through the office door. He knew about Wil's bounty hunting past and had vowed to keep his secret.

"Before I leave, I'd like to look at your dodgers," said Wil.

Logan opened a desk drawer and removed a stack of wanted posters and laid them in front of Wil. One by one, he looked at each poster in turn, setting aside three. When he reached the bottom of the stack, he looked up at Logan Shepherd.

"I found all three."

Logan looked at the three posters. The faces of Wade Jessup, Briley Cole and Jess Walker looked back at him. Logan slid the handbills back to Wil.

Wil folded the posters, put them in his shirt pocket and stood up, holding out his hand to his friend.

"So long, Logan. Keep an eye on Miguel until I get back."

Logan shook Wil's hand.

"Be careful, Wil."

Wil reined up at the white picket fence surrounding the grave of his beloved Cassie. The gravesite sat on a hill under a tree, overlooking the farm. She liked to come up here and sit.

Dismounting, he walked through the gate, picking up the wooden folding chair that lay on the ground next to the fence. He unfolded the chair, sitting down next to the grave. Taking off his hat, he set it on the ground next to the chair.

"I guess you're wondering why I'm dressed in my old clothes again. You prob'ly noticed I was wearin' my gun too. I'm goin' after the scum that done this thing to you. I know I promised you I wouldn't wear a gun again, but I didn't know this would happen, either. Don't be mad, just try to understand. Miguel's gonna watch the farm and I'm takin' Goldie and Buck with me. Goldie's a good horse and Buck'll be a good companion. I don't know how long it will take, but I'll come back every so often to let you know how it's goin'. I love you, Cassie. I always have and I always will."

Wil picked up his hat and put it on. Rising from the chair, he picked it up, folded it and laid it next to the fence as he walked through the gate. Buck was sitting outside the gate and Wil scratched the big brown dog's head as he walked by him.

Mounting the Palomino, Wil sat for a moment, looking at Cassie's grave. Turning the horse, he looked down at Buck.

"Ready to go, boy?"

Buck replied with a boisterous bark, running after Wil.

Long days on the trail gave a man a lot of time to think. Wil Sunday thought about the events that put him on the vengeance trail.

He was a bounty hunter when he walked into the general store in the town of Gunsight. Cassie Landis was the prettiest store clerk he had ever seen. It took some doing, but he finally persuaded her to have dinner with him.

A whirlwind romance ensued and three months later they were married. But first, he had to promise to unstrap his guns. He put the guns and clothes in a trunk that he buried under the hay in the loft of the barn on their newly-bought Kansas farm. That was where the trunk was when the three outlaws rode into his yard, gunned him down and had their way with Cassie before they killed her.

A deep-throated bark from Buck interrupted Wil's thoughts. Ahead of them, six riders circled a tree under which a seventh rider sat mounted with his hands tied behind his back. A rope over the bottom branch of the tree was noosed around his neck.

"Looks like someone's about to get his neck stretched," Wil said to Buck, pulling his Henry rifle from the saddle boot. "You know how I feel about lynchin's."

Wil heeled Goldie and reined up outside the circle of riders.

"Keep ridin', mister, this don't concern you," said the rider nearest to Wil.

Wil held his Henry rifle across his lap. He raised it and rested its stock on his thigh.

"I don't have much of a stomach for lynchin's," said Wil.

"Then, ride on, or you'll take his place," growled a rider from the middle of the circle. He walked his horse to the edge of the circle facing Wil.

Wil figured this was the leader. His graying temples told Wil he was older than the rest. His funneled hat brim tilted forward to shade his eyes.

"I'll ride on when you release the kid," said Wil. He

noticed the intended victim couldn't have been more than eighteen years old. The rider turned and looked at the tree, then back at Wil.

"Looks to me like you ain't in a position to make demands. You're a little outnumbered, I'd say."

"Maybe so. But, you'll be the first one I drop when the shootin' starts."

The rider leaned forward. "I don't think you'll get a shot off."

Wil leveled his Henry at the rider, thumbing back the hammer.

"You willin' to take that chance, mister?"

"You know who I am?"

"Don't matter. Turn the kid loose."

The rider stared at Wil, but Wil's eyes never left the circle of riders. The first sign of trouble would come from them, not the one in front of him.

"Turn 'im loose," yelled the rider, not taking his eyes from Wil.

The rider nearest the kid removed the noose from around his neck and untied his bound hands. As soon as the kid was free, he heeled his horse out of the circle.

"Now, unbuckle your gunbelts," said Wil, as the kid rode out of sight.

"I hope it was worth it, 'cause you just made the biggest mistake of your life," the leader said as he unbuckled his gunbelt and let it fall. Wil watched the gunbelts of the rest of the circle fall to the ground.

"Maybe, maybe not. Now, the rifles." One by one, rifles clattered to the ground.

"Now, ride out."

The rider gave Wil a look of pure hatred. If looks could kill, Wil would have dropped from his saddle.

"You ain't seen the last of me, mister." He spun his horse and rode away at a gallop with the rest of his riders falling in behind him.

When the dust settled and the band of riders were barely visible in the distance, Wil let the hammer down on his Henry rifle and slid it back into its saddle boot. He looked down at Buck.

"Think we can make it to Gunsight without getting in anymore trouble?"

Gunsight was not the quiet town Wil Sunday remembered. It had grown with new buildings along the street. The name McKinney dominated the businesses in the new buildings. He appeared to have a good hold on Gunsight.

A collection of horses marked a new saloon down the street. Wil would see an old friend to find out what went on in Gunsight.

Wil dismounted in front of O'Shay's Saloon. The owner of the saloon, Jimmy O'Shay, a big redheaded Irishman, stood behind the bar wiping glasses. He turned when he heard Wil come through the batwings.

"Are me eyes playin' tricks on me or has Wil Sunday risen from the dead," said Jimmy O'Shay with a big smile. Walking from behind the bar, he greeted Wil with a big hug and waved him toward the bar.

"Come, let Jimmy O'Shay buy ye a drink."

The big redhead went back behind the bar, setting a bottle of Irish whiskey in front of Wil.

"A special drink for a special friend."

Jimmy poured the whiskey into a shot glass in front of Wil and poured one for himself, lifting his glass to Wil.

"May ye be in heaven a long time before the devil knows yer dead."

They threw their shots back and Jimmy refilled the glasses.

"Awful quiet in here for this time of day, ain't it, Jimmy?" asked Wil after looking around the empty saloon. Jimmy's saloon had always been a popular place in Gunsight. He didn't think he'd ever seen it empty.

"A lot of things have changed since ye left, Wil me boy," replied Jimmy.

"This McKinney have anything to do with that? His name seems to be on just about every building in town."

"Jarod McKinney showed up shortly after ye left. Came with a lot of money and bought up a lot of land. Hired a bunch of gunhands to help 'im hold it, then he started on the town. That's 'is saloon across the street. Even the marshal is bought and paid for."

"Tom Draper still the marshal?"

"That 'e is. Never thought I'd see 'im turn on us like 'e did. McKinney's bunch can pretty much do what they want in Gunsight without any fear of the law."

Wil took the posters from his pocket and spread them out on the bar facing Jimmy.

"You seen any of these men in Gunsight?"

Jimmy studied the rough pictures of the men on the posters and slid them back to Wil.

"Three of McKinney's gunhands."

"You're sure?"

"As sure as I am I'm standin' here talkin' to Wil Sunday."

Wil picked up the posters, refolded them and returned them to his pocket.

"They come in town often?"

Jimmy nodded. "Every night. They'll drink 'til they git run out."

Wil held out his hand to Jimmy O'Shay. "You've been a good friend, Jimmy."

"We couldn't believe it when they told us Cassie'd been murdered. We all loved 'er, Wil. I'll do what I can to help ye get who done this to 'er."

Wil touched his fingers to his hat and left O'Shay's Saloon. He stabled Goldie and got a room at the Gunsight Hotel.

Wil removed his gunbelt, hanging it on the bedpost at the head of the bed. Cracking open the window, he lay down on the bed without removing his boots and was asleep before Buck got settled on the floor.

It was dusk when the tinny piano music from the McKinney saloon drifted through the open window, waking Wil. Buck sat up when Wil rose from the bed.

Moving the curtain with his finger, he looked both ways down the street. McKinney's saloon had a full house. He took his gunbelt from the bedpost, buckled it on and thonged down the holster, shifting it until it felt comfortable.

"Let's go get some supper, we have work to do," Wil said to Buck.

It was dark when Wil walked out of the hotel dining room onto the boardwalk. Buck sat up when he saw Wil.

Standing at the edge of the boardwalk, Wil rolled a cigarette, lighting it with a match he struck on the support post. Stepping into the street, he walked toward the Cattleman's Saloon. Buck lay on the boardwalk when Wil went through the batwings. He weaved through the crowded saloon and up to the near end of the polished mahogany bar. The clack of the roulette wheel blended with the tinny notes of the out of tune piano.

He concentrated his attention on the tables with poker games in progress. This is where he would find his prey. He ordered a beer and proceeded to make his rounds of the poker tables.

Jess Walker sat at the third table he passed. He stood at the table looking at Walker until the gunhand looked up at him. After a second, Walker turned his attention back to the game. Walker had no idea who he was. He would wait for the crowd to thin before he made his move.

Wil was sitting at a nearby table when two of the men at Walker's table left their chairs. Wil rose from his table and walked over to stand in front of the bar facing Walker's table. Standing with his feet apart, he balanced his weight.

"Jess Walker, stand up and get what's comin' to you."

Walker looked up at Wil Sunday as men bolted from the line of fire.

"You talkin' to me, mister?" asked Walker.

"Time to pay up for what you done to me and mine," answered Wil.

"What do you say I done?"

Wil was aware that all the attention in the room was turned toward him and Jess Walker.

"You, Wade Jessup, and Briley Cole rode onto my land, gunned me down and raped and killed my wife."

Walker smiled at Wil Sunday.

"I never rode with Wade Jessup."

Wil reached into his shirt pocket, never taking his eyes from Walker. He shook the poster, unfolding it, and held it up for all to see.

"This says different."

The smile left Walker's face. He jumped up from his chair, drawing his Colt as he came up. Wil anticipated Walker's move, drawing his Colt at the first sign of movement.

He fired before Walker could clear leather with his Colt. His shot struck in the chest, knocking him back, sending him toppling over the chair behind him.

Wil walked to the table and looked down at the motionless outlaw. Thumbing the spent shell from his Colt, he replaced it with a fresh one from his gunbelt and holstered his Colt.

The marshal came into the saloon as Wil was picking up the poster from the floor.

"What happened here?"

"Fair fight, marshal," said the bartender, "Walker drew first."

Marshal Tom Draper looked at Wil Sunday and smiled. "Still might not have been a fair fight."

Wil handed the poster to the marshal. "I'll be at the hotel when you get the money." Wil shouldered past Draper and through the batwings.

Wil sat in his hotel room at the small table cleaning his Colt when he heard a knock at his door. Getting up, he went to the door, careful not to stand in front of it.

"Who is it?"

"Tom Draper."

Wil turned the key and cracked open the door.

"Hello, Wil."

Wil opened the door to admit the marshal.

"Back to your old ways, Wil?" asked Draper as he walked past Wil, stopping at the window. He turned when Wil closed the door and walked back to the table.

"This was personal," said Wil. Sitting down at the table, he resumed cleaning his Colt.

"Walker was one of Jarod McKinney's men. He's not going to kiss you for killing him."

"He's also one of the men who killed Cassie," said Wil without looking up.

"McKinney will come looking for you. People expect it."

Wil stopped cleaning his Colt, laid it on the table, looking up at Draper. "I killed a man today that helped kill my wife. If Jarod McKinney comes looking for me, I won't run. I took care of one problem today, two are left. If I have to, I can take care of another."

Tom Draper left the window and started for the door. "I'll have your money for you in the morning. I'd be obliged if you left town after you collected it."

"You runnin' me out of town, Tom?"

"Let's just say I'm tryin' to stop trouble before it starts."

"Then, you better be talkin' to Jarod McKinney, not me. I'll be leavin' Gunsight when I've finished my business here, not before."

Wil picked up his Colt and resumed cleaning it. "Excuse me if I don't show you to the door." Wil didn't look up again until he heard the door latch behind Tom Draper.

The next morning, Wil and Buck stepped off the board-walk in front of the hotel and walked toward the livery. Saddling Goldie, Wil led her across the street, hitching her to the rail in front of the gunsmith.

Stepping up on the boardwalk, Wil opened the door of the gun shop, ringing the bell mounted above the door on a taut spring. Hans Larson, known as Swede, sat at a workbench with his back to the door. He turned on his swivel stool when the bell rang.

"Wil Sunday," said Larson, with a heavy Swedish accent and a big smile. He got up from his stool, circled the glass display case and pumped Wil's hand vigorously. The Swede had been Wil's personal gunsmith when he was hunting bounty, paying regular visits to Gunsight to see him.

"Didn't know if I was going to see you again," said Swede, "They said you was in a bad way."

"Hell, Swede, It's gonna take more than a coupla pieces of lead to stop me."

"You may get a chance to find out. Jess Walker was one of Jarod McKinney's gunhands."

"So I've heard. Everyone keeps tellin' me how much trouble I'm in. Well, Jess Walker was one of them that killed Cassie. I did what I had to do."

"Won't matter to McKinney," said Swede. He held up a finger at Wil and picked up a ring of keys from his workbench, went to a locked cabinet and unlocked it.

"McKinney never goes anywhere without three or four of his gunhands, so let's even it up a little."

Larson took an oilskin bundle from the top shelf of the cabinet and laid it on the glass display case in front of Wil pointing to it.

"Go ahead, open it," said Swede with a grin.

Wil took his Bowie knife and cut the twine around the oilskin, smiling when he unwrapped the bundle.

"I thought I'd seen the last of this."

139

Wil picked up the Greener shotgun. The barrels and stock had been sawed off to make for easier handling. It had been a valuable weapon to Wil in his bounty hunting days. He sold it to Swede when he married Cassie, but Swede couldn't part with it, keeping it cleaned, oiled and wrapped. Now, he was giving it back to its rightful owner.

Swede went back to the cabinet to retrieve the saddle boot that went with it, putting it in front of Wil. He slid the Greener into the boot.

"You may need it sooner than you think," said Swede, nodding to the front window of the shop.

Jarod McKinney rode with three men down the street.

"You have a back door?" asked Wil. Swede pointed to a curtained doorway.

"Through there."

Wil grabbed the Greener and started through the curtain.

"Hey," shouted Swede, tossing Wil a box of shotgun shells. "Gun works better with these."

Wil smiled at Swede, touched two fingers to his hat and slid through the curtain.

Jarod McKinney rode into Gunsight with his foreman, Cinch Riley, and two of his gunhands, Wade Jessup and Briley Cole. They turned into the hitch rail at the Marshal's office and dismounted. Something caught Riley's eye as he stepped down from his saddle and nudged Jarod McKinney as he stepped up on the boardwalk.

"Seen that yeller horse before?" Riley asked McKinney.

"Yeah, I have," replied McKinney and turned to Jessup and Cole.

"Go check out who owns that yeller horse and bring him here to me."

The two gunhands walked across the street and into Swede Larson's shop.

"Where's the fella that owns that purty horse out front?" Jessup said to Larson who was rearranging a gun display. Swede shook his head.

"He didn't come in here."

"Well, we'll just take us a little look around," said Jessup, going behind the counter to look in the room behind Swede.

Briley Cole went to the curtained doorway, slid back the curtain and was greeted by the double-barreled blast of the Greener, hurling him back into the gun shop. Jessup came from the back room with his Colt drawn.

"Didn't come in here, huh?" he said to Swede, hitting him with the barrel of his Colt knocking him to the floor.

Jessup crept over to the narrow doorway, looking down at Cole lying in a twisted heap. Peeking around the corner of the doorway, he saw the back door standing wide open. He eased into the room, stopping at the back door.

Cinch Riley, who bolted from Tom Draper's office at the sound of the shotgun blast, burst through the gun shop door with his Colt drawn. He looked down at the blood beginning to pool around the dead gunman.

"Jessup," shouted Riley.

"Back here," replied Jessup. Riley moved through the narrow doorway and met Wade Jessup at the back door.

"Ol' man said he wasn't here, but he was waiting when Cole come through the curtain. He went out through here."

"See if you can find him, I'll tell McKinney," said Riley. Jessup stepped through the door into the alley. Riley walked back through the gun shop.

"We'll deal with you, old man, when we're done with him,"

Riley said to Swede as he hurried out the door.

Jessup walked cautiously down the alley, checking every doorway and alcove where a man could hide. Passing the stairwell behind the general store, a stack of crates came tumbling down behind him. A double-barreled blast of the Greener caught him as he turned, killing him before he hit the ground.

"Them two won't be killin' any more women," said Wil, running down the alley reloading the Greener.

Cinch Riley and Jarod McKinney looked out the window of the marshal's office at the sound of the second shotgun blast. Riley looked back at McKinney who nodded toward the door.

"Don't come back without him." McKinney watched Riley jog across the street and disappear between two buildings.

"Who is he, Draper?"

"His name is Wil Sunday and he's got you outclassed, Jarod."

"He's caused me a lot of headaches, killed, probably, three of my men and he's gonna pay."

"He's a killing machine, Jarod, and believes if a man's worth shootin', he's worth killin'. If you brace him, he'll leave you lying in the street and walk away."

"We'll see."

Wil Sunday went back through the open door of the gun shop. Hans Larson sat on the stool at the workbench holding a rag to his head.

"You all right, Swede?" asked Wil.

"Jah, will take more than a bump on the head to stop Hans Larson." He removed the bloody rag from his head revealing a small gash on his forehead.

"I'm going to put a stop to this before anymore innocent people get hurt," said Wil. He laid the Greener on the glass display case.

"I'll be back for this."

"Be careful, McKinney's foreman is still out there. They're not above backshootin'."

Wil went to the front door of the gun shop and out onto the boardwalk.

"Well, well, look what just showed up," said Jarod McKinney when he saw Wil come out of the gun shop. Wil stepped into the street, walking toward the marshal's office.

"Let it go, Jarod, you can't beat him," said Draper.

"Watch me."

Tom Draper and Jarod McKinney watched Wil Sunday walk toward them and stop in the middle of the street.

"McKinney, Jarod McKinney."

McKinney smiled at Tom Draper. "Let's not keep him waiting."

McKinney walked out onto the boardwalk followed by Draper. Stepping into the street, McKinney faced Wil Sunday.

"It's over, McKinney. Enough men have died," said Wil.

"You've caused me a lot of embarrassment, Sunday. It ain't over 'til you're face down in the street."

"Then make your play, McKinney."

Mayor Herbert Addison, in his gray suit and derby hat, walked up beside Tom Draper.

"You have to stop this, marshal," said Addison.

"I tried, Herb, it's too late for that now."

McKinney caught movement behind Wil Sunday and saw Cinch Riley come out from beside the gun shop. With his

Colt drawn, Riley moved into the street behind Wil.

Inside the shop, Hans Larson picked up the Greener shotgun from the counter, breaking it open to check the load. He walked from the counter to the door. Buck, who Wil left in the gun shop with Hans, began to bark when Larson thumbed back both hammers of the scattergun.

When Riley turned he saw Larson in the window with the Greener to his shoulder. The split second of surprised hesitation cost Riley his life. He caught both barrels of the scattergun in his chest, sending him flailing backwards into the street.

Surprised by the shotgun blast, Wil ducked, turned aside and took a quick glance behind him in time to see Cinch Riley fall to the ground.

Seeing his chance, McKinney drew his Colt and fired a hurried shot at Wil Sunday. Turning back to McKinney an instant before the rancher fired, Wil dropped to the ground, firing twice.

McKinney stood with a bewildered look on his face, looking down at the growing red stain on the front of his shirt. Looking up at Wil, McKinney dropped to his knees letting the Colt slip from his fingers. He toppled over, face first, into the street.

Buck ran toward Wil as he picked himself up from the street. Wil thumbed the two shells from his Colt, replacing them from his gunbelt. He looked behind him where Hans Larson was walking toward the lifeless Cinch Riley, the barrels of the Greener resting on his shoulder.

Wil walked up to Jarod McKinney, the crimson stain growing around him. He turned the dead rancher over with the toe of his boot. Sightless eyes looked up at the blue sky.

Wil holstered his Colt and, along with Buck, stepped up on the boardwalk in front of Tom Draper and Mayor Addison.

"You have your town back, Mayor. Don't let it get away this time," said Wil. He reached over and took the marshal's badge from Draper's shirt, handing it to the Mayor.

"I think you need a new marshal too."

Wil turned, stepped into the street and walked back to the gunshop. Swede waited for Wil on the boardwalk.

"Works good, too," he said, handing the scattergun back to Wil. Wil offered his hand to Larson.

"Swede, take care of yourself."

"Come back real soon, Wil," said Swede, shaking Wil's hand. Wil looked down at Buck.

"Let's go home, boy."

The End

Terry Alexander –

Terry's first story with Frontier Tales, "Double Event," was chosen as the Best Story of our third issue. It came as no surprise to find our readers liked his tale titled "Split Nose." (See full bio on page 28.)

SPLIT NOSE

Terry Alexander

Trey Dunlap saw the stream through the tree-cover, sunlight reflected off the water's smooth surface. Twilight was hardly an hour away. It would be good to camp by fresh water, get a rabbit or squirrel, eat a hot meal and watch the evening sky. A movement in the underbrush caught his attention. His hand dropped to the pistol at his side. The Nations were well known to host horse thieves and murderers.

A loud commotion came from a thicket of wild plums near the water's edge. He saw the red dots of ripened fruit long before he saw the source of the ruckus. A mouse-gray horse stamped its hooves, pawing at the dirt.

Trey looked at his immediate surroundings, searching for a campfire or an injured rider. On closer inspection, the gelding had traveled a long distance; the dry sweat on its coat gave it a dull unhealthy look. The saddle had slipped, riding under the animal's belly. The stirrups dragged along the ground.

He slipped off the black horse and approached the gelding, unsure how the animal would react.

"Easy fella," he said softly. "I'll have you out of there in a jiffy."

His hand moved slowly, touching the gray's hind leg. His fingers traced the outline of an S burned into the flesh. The muscles rippled beneath the hide, the horse snorted and sidestepped away from his touch.

"Take it easy," he said, his voice low. "Give me a minute and I'll have you loose."

He rubbed the gray's back, moving his hand up the backbone. The horse flinched, its front hooves working the loose earth.

"Just a little more." He patted the gelding's shoulder, rubbing along the neck to the jawbone and down to the reins.

"Almost there," he said. "This is the tricky part."

He tugged the gray's head toward the ground; gaining him enough slack to loosen the reins from the base of the plum tree.

"We're gonna be friends, you and me." He rubbed the animal's nose, finding an old wound that ran from his nostril halfway to the eye.

"I see you found split-nose." A rough voice spoke behind him. "I've been looking for that lunkhead for two days."

Trey froze at the words, his hands moved away from his body. "I ain't stealing this horse. I found him tangled up in the trees."

"Relax; I'm not looking to gun you down. Turn around and let me get a look at you."

"Don't do anything hasty." Trey moved slowly, taking care to keep his hands visible. "Name's Trey Dunlap. I'm traveling up to Colorado. Heard about the gold strike around Cripple Creek."

"Nice country." A huge man held the reins of an equally large roan gelding. "I took a herd of mules up there some months back. Made a good profit from them miners."

"Thought I might try my luck up there." Trey stared at the muzzle of a Spencer Carbine; a nervous tingle ran the length of his spine. "My dad has a repeater like that. He says it's the truest shooting gun he ever owned. You mind pointing it somewhere else?"

"Just wanted to make sure you was friendly. Name's Buck Kincaid. I got a little spread south of here." He pointed the rifle skyward. "It's near dark. What you say we share a camp down by the river? Start out fresh in the morning."

Trey nodded. "That sounds good to me." He offered Buck the reins. "Here's your horse. I wasn't trying to steal it."

"You don't know, do you?" Buck frowned.

"Know what?"

"That ugly thing belongs to Orville Summers. He's offered fifty dollars to the man who brings it home."

"Where can I find this fella? I could use fifty dollars."

A smile broke Buck's face. "You up to an even split?"

Trey returned the grin. "Sure, twenty-five's better than nothing."

"He's got a ranch about three days south of here. Let's fix that saddle and get down to the creek to give these animals water and rest."

"What happened to its nose?" Trey asked as he moved the saddle to an upright position.

"Heard it was a snake bite. One of the ranch hands had the bright idea to lance it and left the animal scarred for life." Buck slipped the Spencer into the scabbard. "Damn horse ain't good for much. Doesn't have any cattle sense at all. He's a straight-line animal. Put him on the trail and he can walk any other horse in the ground.

"Summers's got a little money. Got a ranch down on the Red River, Texas side. Does pretty fair for himself."

Trey looped his rope over the gray's head and tied it off to his saddle horn. "This animal ain't worth ten dollars, tops," in one motion he swung into the black's saddle. "It doesn't make any sense for him to pay fifty dollars for it."

"Orville's a strange man. He takes things real personal. He trailed a man for a week once when the fella cheated him in a poker game. Gave him the beating of his life and left him afoot on the trail."

"Sounds like a hard man." Trey tugged on the reins, moving the black toward the stream.

"He ain't a man to take for granted. Orville came here after the war, got a piece of land and spread out over the years. Split Nose belongs to his boy, Grant. The boy lost it about a week ago. I don't know all the details."

"There's some raw spots around its legs and belly."

"I've got some salve in my saddlebags. We'll doctor them sores before we turn in." Buck nodded. "I've also got some salted middlin and a spot of coffee. We can have a pretty good supper."

"Sounds good to me. I've been eating jerky for two days."

"There's good grass here for the horses." Buck rode to the waters edge; the roan dipped its mouth to the smooth surface, filling its belly.

The leather creaked as Trey removed his saddle. The strong odor of dried horse sweat drifted up from the blanket. He laid the saddle with the underside to the sky to allow it to air overnight.

"How you gonna spend your share of the money?" Buck asked as he scavenged for wood.

"I've got a weakness for poker. Thought I might use it for seed money, maybe add to it." Trey laughed. "Miners aren't very good poker players. What about you?"

"I owe Ben Ross a little money down at the general store. After I pay him off, I'm gonna stock up on supplies, and then I'm gonna get something nice for Rachel and Emily. That's my wife and baby."

"Let me gather up the firewood." Trey offered. "While you doctor on Split-nose. Just lay out the fixin's and I'll be back directly."

"I'll be here." Buck rummaged through his belongings for the ointment.

Trey staggered back to the campsite a short time later burdened with a large load of wood. "I tried to get enough to last out the night." He dumped the sticks on the ground. "I like to keep a fire going."

Buck remained silent.

"Something wrong?" Trey asked.

"That horse has had a rough life. It's got a lot of old scars and nicks on his flanks and legs."

Trey glanced at the animals munching on a patch of grass. "Not our business," he said. "Let's just take it home and collect our money."

"Those marks couldn't have happened natural. It ain't right."

"Don't think about that horse. Think about your wife and kid. Twenty-five dollars can ease your conscience."

"Maybe so." Buck nodded. "But money ain't everything. Some things are more important."

"Right now, we both need money. Keep that in mind."

Buck's lips thinned into a hard line. He dug the salted meat and coffee out of his saddlebags.

This is crazy. Trey arranged the wood for the cooking fire. He's worrying about a broomtail that don't even belong to him. The silence grew between the two men. Dawn seemed a long way off.

They arrived at the Summers ranch late on the third day. Nice place, Trey thought. Two story house, real glass windows, huge barn for the draft animals. This Orville Summers sure knows his business.

A few ranch hands worked around the barn, mending harness or shaping horseshoes on the anvil for the Belgians in the small corral. A thin raw-boned man rose from a raw-hide porch chair and met them in front of the house.

"Are you Mr. Summers?" Trey asked pulling the black to a stop.

The man stared at the pair through red-rimmed eyes. "You found Split-nose."

"Yes sir, just north of the Red." Buck nudged his horse up to the old man. "Remember me? I used to work for you, Mr. Summers, about three years ago. Name's Buck Kincaid."

The old man failed to acknowledge Buck's greeting. "I never figured he'd swim the river." Summers dabbed at his eyes with a handkerchief.

"I tracked him for two days." Buck nodded his head. "Time I caught up with him, Trey had already found him."

"Buck told me about the reward, so we started this way double quick." Trey swung from the saddle, the dry dust puffed up from under his boot sole.

"Reward?" Summers stared vacantly at the two men.

"Fifty dollars." Buck cleared his throat. "You offered fifty dollars to anyone who brought Split-nose home."

"That's right, fifty dollars." Summers turned toward the house. "Grant died four days ago," he mumbled as he stepped up on the rough planks. "We buried him yesterday."

"What did he say?" Trey turned to Buck. "Did you hear him?"

"Something about Grant and a funeral. I think his boy died."

"Damn, I hate to hear that. I wonder if he still wants the horse."

"He'll pay. Orville Summers always keeps his word," Buck looked at the outbuildings and corrals. "One day I'll have a place like this."

"Grant didn't check his cinch strap." Summers said, as he returned. The sound of his voice startled both men. "He was showing off like boys his age do, trying to impress the young girls." The old man stood quiet for several seconds.

"Mr. Summers, are you . . . ?" Trey asked to break the silence.

"I'm fine." Summers's eyes popped open. He wiped at his nose. "I owe you boys some money," he said, as he passed each man a handful of crumpled bills.

Trey stuffed his share in his shirt pocket. "Thanks, Mr. Summers. I'm sorry about your son."

"Grant was a good boy," Buck said. "He would have been a man to be proud of."

"Freda named him after her pa." Summers looked toward the horizon. "She's been sitting at the kitchen table since the funeral, just sips at her coffee, won't say nary a word."

"We won't trouble you any longer." Trey's boot slipped into the stirrup. His hand circled the saddle horn; he pulled himself aboard.

"We'll leave you to your grieving." Buck touched his fingers to his hat brim.

"He loved this sorry horse," Summers mumbled. "Used to brag about how much ground it could cover in a day. Freda blames Split-nose for Grant's death. She thinks it meant to kill him."

Trey stared at the black's ears, unwilling to make eye contact with the older man. "I know it doesn't seem possible now, but she'll come around. She'll get to thinking about the good times."

"Not with Split-nose around. Every time she sees him she'll think of Grant lying in his coffin with his skull bashed in."

Trey wanted to comment. He sat silent for several seconds, searching his mind for the right words, something to comfort Orville. Faster than Trey thought possible the old man pulled a small .36 caliber Remington from his waistband. He placed it two inches from the animal's forehead.

"Don't!" Trey shouted. His spurs touched the black's flanks, urging him forward.

The thunder from the small caliber weapon echoed in the distance. Trey felt a warm splash on his face, as blood splattered his cheek. Split-nose stumbled sideways and crumpled to the ground, its hooves pawing at the earth.

"I had to do it. Don't you see that?" He stood stoop shouldered, looking down at the dying gelding. "I couldn't let Split-nose live, not with Grant dead. I just couldn't let him live."

Trey swallowed the lump in his suddenly dry throat. "Take this, Buck," he fished the bills from his shirt pocket. "I don't want money that bad."

Buck took the bills from Trey's hand. "I don't want it either," he said, shaking his head. "I'll figure out a way to get by." He urged his mount up to Summers. "Take your money. It's tainted."

Summers turned a tear-stained face to the pair. His hand closed on the wad of greenbacks as Split-nose ceased his death throes and lay still. "You understand, don't you? Can't you see I had to kill him?"

Trey sank his spurs into the black's flanks, he had to get away from this place of death and Colorado beckoned.

The End

J. B. Hogan –

J. B. Hogan writes fiction and poetry and local history articles. He plays upright bass in a family acoustic band.

His story, "Ozark Beats," read for the NPR program *Tales from the South* on KUAR, Little Rock, Arkansas, is also streamed on the internet and is available on World Radio stations. The video of the reading can be seen on You Tube and Facebook. "Train Boarding" (fiction) was selected as one of "The Best of the Cynic Online Magazine 2010" and his poem "The Classic Age" won Second Place in The Medulla Review Oblongata Contest #3, August 2010.

His flash fiction piece, "Kerosene Heat," was nominated for a 2010 Pushcart Prize by Word Catalyst and his flash fiction piece, "Janey," won First Place in The Medulla Review Oblongata Contest #4, September 2010. His dystopian novel, *New Columbia,* was a "Best of Long Fiction 2009" selection by Aphelion and his poem, "Gray Man," was selected as one of "The Best Pieces of 2009" by Cynic Online Magazine.

"Waiting for Jesus," published in the Dead Mule, was selected as one of the storySouth Million Writers Award Notable Stories of 2009 and his 2008 prize-winning fiction e-book, *Near Love Stories,* is online at Cervena Barva Press. He has three stories in Flash of Aphelion, a print-on-demand anthology, May 2010. In addition, he has published some 200 stories and poems in such journals as *Istanbul Literary Review, Every Day Poets, Ranfurly Review, Smokebox, Bewildering Stories*, and *Avatar Review.*

LAST RIDER: NOPAL, TEXAS

by J. B. Hogan

When Moses Traven crossed over into the Territory from Fort Smith, he had every intention of avoiding the Boston Mountains in the north of Arkansas. He planned to skirt those hard-to-ride hills and the rest of the Ozarks altogether until picking up the old trail in southwest Missouri that led to the one-time trailhead town of Sedalia. Mose hoped there might still be work there.

During his first full day out of Fort Smith, however, Mose's plans changed – and changed quick. From out of nowhere, an early norther blew up across the flat lands of the Territory and drove him south towards Texas.

Riding into the little town of Nopal at daybreak, the norther still on his heels, Mose headed Buster, his dependable buckskin, for the usual place he figured he could hole up and ride out the weather – the local livery stable. Remembering the kindness of Henry Hallow, the blacksmith and stable man back in Fort Smith, Mose hoped the Nopal smithy would run just as friendly an establishment. It turned out be a false hope.

"One dollar a night," this blacksmith grunted, not even looking at Mose, who had reached his hand out for shaking.

"You sleep on the hay you feed your animal."

"One dollar?" Mose questioned.

"Take it or leave it," the blacksmith said. Mose turned Buster to go. "Six-bits." Mose kept Buster moving. "Four-bits." Mose reined in Buster and backed him up.

"Clean hay for my horse and for me."

"Suit yourself. Four-bits."

Mose dug in his shirt pocket and came up with the money.

"Put the animal in the middle stall across there," the blacksmith said curtly.

"That'll do," Mose said, nodding his head.

What a difference between good old Henry in Fort Smith and this character. The man still hadn't even looked at Mose, much less introduced himself or asked who Mose was.

After unsaddling Buster and giving him a good currying, Mose climbed up to the stable loft and found some clean hay to lay his bedroll on. He dug in his saddle bags for some jerky he'd bought in Fort Smith and after eating a couple of chunks of it, lay down for a rest.

Around dusk the smith stopped his banging and clanging below and left the stable. Mose tried to sleep but it was just too early. Instead he closed his eyes and daydreamed about riding a wide, sure-footed trail into a land of high green grass and tall thick trees. He could see a small creek running alongside the trail and there were small mountains, not much more than hills, in the blue distance and a –

Suddenly, Mose opened his eyes, quickly out of his daydream. Someone was in the stable below.

It had turned dark and Mose couldn't see the floor or stables very well but he heard Buster snort and dig at the ground with his hooves. Carefully reaching for his .36

caliber Navy revolver in its holster beside the bedroll, Mose took the weapon and quietly moved up to the edge of the loft. There was someone stirring below. Mose aimed his pistol at the figure and called down, "Who's there? What are you doing?"

The figure stopped moving but there was no answer. Mose made a production out of cocking the .36.

"Wait, wait," a high voice cried out. "Don't shoot. I'm the smithy's wife."

"What are you doing down there?" Mose asked.

"Come to see if you was hungry," the woman answered. "Got some food here."

Mose heard a scratching on one of the stable's wood beams and then a match flared. The woman lit an oil lamp she carried and set it on a work table.

"Biscuits and bacon," she called up to Mose. "Figured you might like some."

"Yes, ma'am," Mose said, holstering the .36 before hustling down out of the loft.

In the light of the lamp, the smithy's wife looked to be several years her husband's junior. She had long brown hair, flowing wild and free, and sharp, playful brown eyes. Her skin was dark and smooth, with a narrow attractive nose above her full mouth – which seemed always on the verge of forming into a laughing sneer. Her long, form-fitting cotton dress left little doubt as to her womanly attributes, which Mose tried to ignore.

"I reckon you was some hungry," she said, watching Mose tear after the food.

From the little curl in the woman's well-defined lips, it looked like she might have more to say on the subject – on any subject for that matter.

"I reckon I was," Mose said, concentrating on consuming his meal.

He didn't think the smithy would necessarily cotton to his wife being out in the stable chatting with Mose after dark – whether it was to bring him food or not.

"There's water here, too," the woman said, pointing to a small cup beside the cloth she'd brought the biscuits and bacon in.

"'Preciate it," Mose replied, taking a swig of the water with his last bite of food. "How much I owe you?"

"You don't owe me nothin'," the woman said, moving up close to Mose to retrieve the food cloth.

Mose downed the rest of the water and handed her the cup. Her hand grazed his during the exchange. It felt like lightning running through Mose's body. The woman moved closer yet. She was so close, Mose could feel the warmth of her body and the smell of something sweet on her breath. He suppressed an urge to put his arm around her waist.

"I better get back up in the loft," he said, rising quickly. Just as he did, the blacksmith came banging through the back door of the stable.

"What the hell is goin' on out here?" he bawled at Mose and his wife.

"Whoa," Mose said, instinctively backing up. "Nothin's goin' on."

"You get back in the house," the smithy growled at his wife.

The woman turned and with a lovely sneer for both Mose and her husband, sashayed right out of the stable as if she were a noble lady strolling in a manicured English garden.

The smithy glowered at her retreating figure and when she was gone turned his harsh glare on Mose.

"Stay away from my woman," he said coarsely, "if you know what's good for you."

"I wasn't doin' nothin' with your woman," Mose countered, "and I wasn't intendin' to."

"You saddle tramps think you can just come in anywhere and take what you want," the man said.

"I don't think no such thing," Mose shot back, "and I'd be goin' easy on the saddle tramp part."

"I'll say what I . . . ." the smithy began, but stopped when he saw Mose square up into a fist-fighting position. "I . . . just don't like nobody messin' with my wife."

"I done told you I wasn't messin' with nothin'," Mose said, making no effort to conceal his anger or lack of respect for the pushy smithy.

The smithy looked Mose up and down, saw the hard, clenched fists, the fire in the eyes, the position ready to strike. He backed away. Slowly, but surely, snatching the lamp off the work table where his wife had left it.

When the troublesome man was gone, Mose let out a deep breath and relaxed his hands and body. Seemed like these days somebody was always trying to start something with him. In the dark of the stable he climbed back up into the loft to his bedroll and lay down to try and get a night's sleep. He kept the .36 nearby just in case.

Mose woke next morning to a commotion in the road outside the stable. Sleepy-eyed and still groggy from his long run on Buster away from the recent storm, he slowly raised himself up and peered over the loft edge. The blacksmith was there already, preparing for his day's work.

"What's all that ruckus out there?" Mose called down.

"You cowboys are mighty slow for risin', I reckon," the blacksmith said by way of answer.

"Don't concern me no how," Mose dismissed the topic.

"If you have to know," the smithy said grumpily, "they was a stagecoach robbery yesterday. The guard was winged and a passenger shot and killed."

"My God," Mose said, "that's terrible."

"Hmph," the smithy grunted.

The conversation seemingly over, Mose put on his boots and started gathering his gear. There didn't seem any reason to stay in this place any longer, especially now that the norther had passed through. Down in the stable, he fed and watered Buster. The smithy acted like he was busy but he was keeping track of every movement Mose made.

"Leaving in a hurry?" the smithy finally said, unable to restrain a natural impulse towards nosiness.

"Yeah," Mose answered, "I don't see any – ."

Before Mose could finish his sentence, the doors of the stable swung open and several men marched in. At their head was a big man wearing a star.

"Morning, Enoch," the lawman spoke to the smithy, while giving Mose a quick once-over.

"Morning, marshal," Enoch said, also giving Mose a fast glance. Mose tossed and straightened the blanket on Buster's back in preparation for saddling him.

"I reckon 's you heard about the stagecoach?" the marshal asked the smith.

"Yes, sir," Enoch said firmly. "Got you a killer on your hands. A loner was it?"

"One man," the marshal confirmed. "Shot the guard, killed a passenger. Rode on towards Nopal, the driver said."

"Anybody else get it?" Enoch asked.

"No, thankfully," the marshal said. "A woman and man, not together, were unhurt. The other poor fella got it in the neck. Bled to death out there."

Enoch didn't say anything but he turned his head in Mose's direction, enough so to make the marshal do the same. Mose was tossing the saddle onto Buster's back.

"What about you, young fella?" the marshal spoke to Mose. "What's your story?"

"My story?" Mose asked.

"Yeah, where you from? Where you headin' in such a hurry."

"I ain't in a hurry," Mose said evenly, giving Enoch a cold stare, "I'm just leavin'. Ain't the most hospitable place I seen."

"Where were you late yesterday?"

"Ridin' into here."

"He come in right about after that shootin'," Enoch volunteered. "Come off the trail. He's a saddle tramp. He might be your man."

"You son of a –," Mose began.

"Easy, son," the marshal said, squaring up towards Mose. Some of the men with the lawman did the same. Mose stopped saddling Buster. "We just need to ask you a few questions."

"It's him," Enoch said, wagging a finger at Mose. "I know it is. He paid me with brand new coins. Bet he got 'em from the strongbox on the coach. Hell, yes. I knew they was somethin' wrong with him right away. Scared my wife in the night, too. Damn near raped her, I figure."

"Why you lyin' dog," Mose growled, stepping forward menacingly towards Enoch. The smithy took refuge behind the marshal's delegation.

"Hold up, boy," the marshal ordered Mose. He pointed his finger at Mose and two of his biggest men grabbed Mose who started to struggle, then thought better of it.

"You're makin' a big mistake, marshal," Mose said, red-faced, "this lyin' weasel made all that stuff up."

"We'll decide that," the marshal said, "over at the office. You come along peaceful, son, or we'll take you there the hard way."

"I ain't done nothin'," Mose insisted, but he went along quietly. There was nothing else for it.

The Nopal city jail was not much more than a cage at the back of the tiny marshal's office. There was only one rickety wooden cot with a filthy, lice-infested mattress that could have doubled for a worn-out blanket it was so thin. Mose ended up putting the mattress under the cot, finding hard wood more comfortable than the insect-filled padded cloth.

Well into late afternoon, after leaving Mose pretty much to his own devices for the better part of the day, the marshal, a thick-headed deputy, and some man named Carlton who had something to do with the local court bustled into the jail with news for Mose.

"We found your stash of loot, boy," this Carlton blustered, as the three men gathered around Mose's cage.

"I ain't got no stash of loot," Mose said tiredly.

"What do you call this, then?" the thick-skulled deputy asked. He held up Mose's twenty dollar gold-piece and the remaining paper money he had left.

"I call that wages," Mose replied.

"Nobody makes that much money," Carlton countered.

"We found it among your belongings, son," the marshal said.

"Look, marshal," Mose said, feeling the marshal might be a good bit more reasonable than the deputy and the court man, "I earned that money. Ridin' trail."

"That gold-piece is spankin' new," the deputy said. "Like it came off that strongbox from the robbery." Mose shook his head. These boys weren't listening.

"Why you hidin' that money, if you earnt it?" Carlton huffed.

"Why do you think?" Mose said.

"You stole it, that's why," the deputy shot back.

"I'm on the trail these days," Mose explained patiently, "you can't leave what you got out in the open."

"Where were you headed?" the marshal asked.

"Sedalia," Mose answered.

"Sedalia?" Carlton laughed. "Boy, you are a liar. You come in from the north, the smithy said he seen that. You goin' the wrong direction if you was goin' up to Missouri."

"I was tryin' to outrun the norther," Mose said. "You call me a liar again and I'll come out of here and knock your head off, mister."

"See, marshal," Carlton squealed, jumping back away from the cell, "he's the one. He's the killer. He's threatenin' to kill me. For nothin'."

"Take it easy, son," the marshal told Mose.

"I'm tellin' you, marshal," Mose said with some heat, "I never had nothin' to do with no stagecoach robbin' nor killin'. And I don't like bein' called a liar by some damned polecat."

"You'll think polecat," Carlton spat at Mose, while backing towards the jail door. "You killed a good man. A good man from this town. People knew him good. You'll pay for this. People in town will see to that. You'll pay soon."

"Calm down, Carlton," the marshal said. "Judge Winter will be here in a couple of days, he'll decide."

"There may not be nothin' to decide by then," Carlton threatened, opening the jail door. "There won't be no need for a trial."

"Go on," the marshal told him.

"Mark my words," Carlton called back from the doorway, "it'll be settled long before that."

After Carlton, the would-be vigilante, left the jail, Mose tried to calm his own nerves by lying down and resting for a bit. He stretched out carefully on the wood slats of the cot, his feet dangling off one end and closed his eyes. He tried to picture in his mind what his parents looked like but too many other images from the last ten years of his life gained the forefront and he could not clearly picture either his mother's or his father's face.

He could remember the handful of battles he'd been in when serving under General Shelby in Missouri. Boonville, Waverly, the bitter defeat at Westport. The retreat and collapse of General Price's command. The flight into Mexico and the mixed experience in the Carlota colony. It was there –

Of a sudden it seemed, Mose was startled awake by loud shouting outside the jail. Sitting up quickly, he was surprised to see it had gotten completely dark. The unseen mob was loud and boisterous but Mose could occasionally hear the marshal's voice over the general clamor. He was sure he heard Carlton and maybe Enoch as well.

"He killed Bert," Carlton's voice declared into the night.

"Kill him," came a chorus of angry voices.

"Take it easy now," the marshal counseled the mob.

"Bert was our friend," someone cried.

"He was mine, too," the marshal allowed, "but lynchin' this fellow without a trial ain't right."

"We want him," someone else demanded, "now." Mose thought it might have been Enoch.

The next outburst from the crowd was unintelligible and Mose's attention was then drawn to a nearer, different sound. It was a hissing noise coming from the back of the cell. He got up from the cot and walked back to the barred window to find its source. At the window, he was shocked to see Enoch's pretty young wife just outside the back of the jail.

"What are you doin' there?" Mose asked her.

"I got your horse," the woman said, "I'm gonna bust you out of there before they hang you."

"What?" Mose wondered, almost laughing. "What are you talking about?" But when he looked outside more carefully, he could see the woman had Buster saddled and ready to go.

"Here," the woman said, reaching the end of a thick rope inside the jail to Mose. "Knot that around the window bars. This adobe ought to fall apart like dry sand with a good pull."

"Are you crazy, woman?" Mose said, holding the end of the rope like it was a dirty yellow rattlesnake. "I'm under arrest. I gotta wait for the judge to come. There's gonna be a trial when he gets here. I'll be let go. They'll see I'm innocent."

"They'll see you're hung is more like it," the woman shot back. "You ain't gonna make it through the night much less till the judge gets here."

Mose listened to the loud, unintelligible sounds of the vigilante crowd outside the front of the jail. The woman had a point.

"You got that rope tied good to the saddlehorn on Buster?" Mose wanted to know.

"I will," the woman said, "on one condition."

"Oh, no," Mose groaned.

"You gotta take me with you."

"Hell, woman, I'll be lucky if I make it a mile out of town even if we do pull this window out. They'll be comin' hell bent for me, lickety-split."

"I cain't stay here. Enoch beats me. He's a God-awful man, mister."

"If I take you, we both die," Mose said flatly. "Buster cain't carry the both of us."

"He looks big and strong."

"Not that big and strong."

"Hell."

"Listen, lady, I thank you truly for helpin' me, but I gotta go alone. There's no other way."

The woman was silent. Mose listened to the mob out front. It was getting louder. There was no time to lose.

"Bust me out, woman, or forget about it," Mose said. "It's dark out there, run off the other side. Nobody'll see you. That old man of yours won't know you did it."

"Damn it, mister."

"I'm sorry."

"Damn," the woman repeated, but she made sure the rope

knot on the saddlehorn was as tight as she could get it.

Mose hooked his end around each of the two bars closest to where he stood. They looked the weakest. He tied the rope off tight.

"Swat Buster on the rear. Hard," Mose told her, "he's strong."

The woman did as she was told and Buster gave a leap forward, straining against the rope and the wall it and he was attached to. The lady swatted the horse again and he pulled hard against his restraints. The barred window ground out on the side closest to Mose and with a hard kick he knocked two chunks of adobe wall loose. Buster jerked forward again with another slap on the rear and the wall separated enough for Mose to climb through. He was out. Free.

"God bless you, lady," he said, pulling the knotted rope loose from the window bars.

The woman gave Mose a quick hug, shoved a pistol into his hand and dropped something round and shiny into his shirt pocket. Without another word she disappeared into the darkness. Mose could hear the crowd going wild in front. They'd heard the noise. He didn't have much time.

Sticking the pistol behind his belt, he ran to Buster, clambered into the saddle and dug his heels into the horse's sides. The spirited animal practically leaped forward, then galloped into the desert night, Mose pleading for more speed as they shot out of the little town and onto the stagecoach road.

Behind them, the mob cursed and yelled, fired wildly and inaccurately in the general direction of the escapees. None of the rounds even came close to them, but Mose kept Buster at a gallop until he was sure they were completely out of range.

He ran the animal as fast and hard as he dared in the available light.

About a mile or so outside Nopal, they left the stagecoach road and headed due north toward the Big Dipper, toward the refuge of Indian Territory, toward freedom. When Mose could no longer hear anything but the normal sounds of night, he reined Buster in and let him cool down at a reasonable walking pace.

The night was still, reassuringly quiet. Mose was sorry he had had to leave the lady back there to deal with her vicious husband and the mindless mob, but there was nothing he could do about it. They were looking to string him up. He had to escape.

As the night deepened into its darkest hours, man and horse were one in the opaque shadows. Nopal was well in the distance now. Mose kept on a northerly trail, he never once looked back.

The End

John Putnam –

John graduated from U.C. Berkeley with a degree in music but found a laptop keyboard more his forte than a piano. He has an ardent interest in history and his recently completed novel, *Hangtown Creek*, a story of adventure, romance, and coming of age that unfolds in the early days of the California Gold Rush, is available online from Amazon and Barnes and Noble.

To read a healthy sample of *Hangtown Creek* or discover John's informative online articles on the rich history of the gold rush please visit his web site at www.goldrushtales.com.

BOTTOMLESS BARTLETT'S BEAUTIFUL BRIDE

John Putnam

I stood there idly wiping clean glasses with a dirty bar rag and watching my only customer shovel food down his maw like a hungry grizzly bear after a long winter nap. Bottomless Bartlett they called him and the man could pack enough grub away in one day to feed Kearny's Army of the West for a week. He ate all the time and never seemed to get enough. No doubt he was a big fellow, at least a head taller than anyone in San Francisco and not an ounce of fat on him. Bartlett was as fit as a fiddle and proud of it.

Six eggs scrambled together with hot chili peppers, four pork chops each half as thick as your little finger is long, a loaf of fresh bread smothered in a pound of butter, three plates of refried Mexican beans, all washed down with a pot of coffee and five pints of beer. Now, if all that wasn't enough, he hollered for my cook to bring him dessert. Right away Rafael burst out the kitchen door with a plate full of apple pan dowdy and Bartlett dug right in like he hadn't seen food in a month.

"Bartlett, why don't you find a good woman and settle

173

down? You could save a small fortune just eating at home," I said, knowing as soon as the words passed my lips that I had stepped in a deep pile of fresh horse leavings.

"Aw, Willie, you know there ain't no woman around gonna marry me. Heck, I just ain't good looking enough for any of the gals I know."

There it was. The south end of a northbound mule looked better than Bartlett and had more brains to boot. His ears were too big, his nose too small, his muddy brown hair had never met a brush or a comb and lay on his head like a rat's nest on top of the gnarly stump of a broken down pine tree. Bartlett was as homely as they come.

But I'd already stepped in it. I had to keep going no matter how much it stank. "You spent two years in the gold country, Bartlett. Can't you cook for yourself?"

"Never got much past bacon and flapjacks," he mumbled, his mouth full of pie.

"Well, there ought to be one woman in this town you'd take a fancy to," I said before I'd thought. There must be ten or twenty men for every gal in town. If any one of them wanted to get married, and most didn't, they had their choice – and ugly Bottomless Bartlett wouldn't be at the top of any girl's wish list.

"Aw, Willie, them women is always talking at me, ordering me around. Even when I was a kid, with my Ma and three older sisters, it was Bartlett do this, Barlett don't do that. Day after day they'd nag at me, run me ragged – dang near drove me batty. Finally I packed up and left for California. Ain't met no woman here who didn't want to boss me around like an old plow horse either."

I couldn't help but think that was because he was dumber

than that old plow horse but thankfully had the good sense not to say so. "Surely there must be one –"

"No, Willie, not that I've met. Heck, having a wife who could cook and who loved me without having to yap all the time would make me as happy as a honey bee in clover. I'd give a hundred dollars – no, I'd give two hundred dollars – to anyone who found the right gal for me. But it ain't no use. There's no woman living who'd go for a guy like me." He stuffed the last of the pie down his throat, swilled a whole glass of beer in one swallow, belched loud then pushed his chair back from the table with a screech.

"Wait up, Bartlettt. Two hundred dollars you say?" I asked, never one to let easy money pass me by with the seeds of an idea already rattling around in my head.

"Yeah, Willie, two hundred dollars – in gold," he said as he burped again.

"Consider yourself married then," I vowed without the foggiest notion that I could pull off the hare-brained scheme that lurked in the dark corners of my greedy brain. But two hundred in gold was a pretty fair reward for what I had in mind – even if I had to split it with someone else.

"Rafael," I yelled and the kitchen door swung open quickly. Rafael had been listening to my conversation with Bartlett, as usual.

"Si, Señor," he said, a knowing smile lifting the corners of his bushy moustache.

"Take care of the bar for me. I got to run down to Pike Street. I'll be back before the noon time crowd gets in."

"Pike Street, Señor? It is too early for the ladies, no?"

"This is business, Rafael, not pleasure."

"Oh, si, si, funny business with the ladies, I comprendez.

Rafael will tend the bar." His smug grin said that he hadn't believed a word I said about doing business on Pike. I ignored him and hurried out the door. After all, two hundred dollars was two hundred dollars.

I walked west on Clay Street for a block and a half then turned south into a small alley lined with Chinese push carts selling vegetables and fruit. Halfway to Sacramento Street I knocked loud at the door of a two-story wood frame house where all the windows were shuttered tight. When no one answered I pounded on it again, louder, and hollered. "Open up, Jasper. I ain't got all day."

In the blink of a gnat's eye the heavy oak door creaked opened and a tall man in a checkered vest peered out, his face as black as a lump of coal. "Mistah Willie, it's way too early fo' th' ladies. Cain't ya wait till noon?" he said.

I pushed my way inside and he closed the door behind me. "I ain't here for a gal, Jasper. I need to see to see the boss lady toot sweet. I reckon she's up and about."

"Why yessah, Mistah Willie. She up but she don't see customers no mo'."

"I know that. But this is business. I got a deal she can't pass on. Go tell her it's Wildcat Willie Wingett and I got a hundred dollars in gold for her."

"Yessah, Mistah Willie. I'll sees if she decent." Jasper left for the back of the house while I nosed about in the parlor wondering why the Madame of one of the biggest bordellos in San Francisco would worry about being decent.

Then the wide double doors to the dining room swung open and the lady of the house swept into the room. Standing all of four foot something from the tips of her dainty toes to the top of her ink black hair piled up high on her head and held together with an ivory comb and a couple of those sticks the Chinese use instead of forks, she looked stunning, as usual, her face powdered as white as the parson's soul, her lips as red as a fresh strawberry. Clad only in a floor-length robe that looked like somebody's calico quilt outfitted with fancy braids and big ivory buttons, Madame Ah Hoi carried a mighty punch in a tiny package.

"You, why you here? Too early. No lookee. No feelee. No –"

"That ain't why I come, Ah Hoi," I interjected before she bit my head off. "I got a deal for you."

"No! No deal. Last time you try pay me brass – no gold. Go way!"

Clearly she hadn't forgotten my little accident, but . . . I smiled innocently.

"Now that was just a big mistake." I explained. "Besides you got your gold. We're square now. Let's let bygones be bygones."

"You be gone, chop chop!" She waved a dismissive hand at me. From the nasty scowl on her face I felt lucky she didn't have a knife.

"Hold on now. Just listen. You got a gal here that ain't working out." I scratched my head. What did Jasper tell me that girl's name was? Hadn't seemed important last week. Oh yeah. "Her name's Sue something –"

"Su Li," she said, suddenly interested. "Why you want Su Li. She not happy here. No good for business. She ugly – feet too big. Men no like. Now all she do cook."

Yes! I thought, one down one to go. "Can she speak English," I ask, eyes wide.

"Su Li Chinee. Why you care?"

"Because Su Li is perfect. Listen, I can marry her off and you and me can get a hundred dollars each in pure gold. Whatta ya say?"

Now Ah Hoi's eyes were sparkling. She leaned in closer. She was interested. "One hundred dollar, real gold – no funny money?" She sure didn't want to let that little thing with the brass filings go.

"No! No funny money. Real gold. One hundred dollars." I assured her.

"Hokay, I listen. What I do for gold?"

It took me the better part of that morning to explain the whole thing to Ah Hoi. She kept saying that Su Li was too ugly and no man would want her because of her big feet, but I finally got it through that thick pile of black hair that must have been plugging her ears that Bottomless Bartlett didn't care one fig about Su Li's feet. He was interested in other things, like her cooking and that she couldn't nag him half to death speaking only Chinese. Finally Jasper jumped in and helped me explain, but only after I had promised him a bottle of my best liquor. Still it was worth it if everything worked out.

The next day I got to the saloon earlier than I had in years. From the incredible aroma that swept in from the kitchen, everything was going exactly as planned. I walked behind the bar, popped a cork and poured myself a tumbler full of rye. It looked like a real profitable day coming.

The front door swung open at exactly five after eight and Bottomless Bartlett breezed in looking as dumb as ever, rainwater dripping from his India rubber overcoat.

"Morning, Bartlett," I said, trying to act nonchalant and not spill the beans.

"Howdy, Willie. Fine day, ain't it?" Bartlett went on.

"As fine as we've had in a while, except for this cold rain and that nasty north wind," I answered and poured him a glass of beer.

He sat at his usual table just as the kitchen door popped open and Rafael appeared, a tray balanced over his head. With a flourish he plopped the platter on a table and whipped off a plate of dumplings and stuck it in front of Bartlett. I could see the big oaf's smile bust out across his ugly mug from way behind the bar.

"You got a new cook, Willie?" he asked, eyes bulging.

"Sorta," I answered. "You like Chinese?" I asked, already knowing the answer.

Bartlett nodded greedily then stuck a fork full of dumplings in his face.

I drained the rest of my rye. "That smells good," I said, but Bartlett ain't listening.

He had the plate clean faster than a good hound dog can tree a coon but Rafael was ready with a jumbo bowl of soup. Bartlett didn't even drop his fork. He just grabbed a spoon in his left hand and had at it. Next came a simmering serving of fresh bay shellfish over a bed of steamed rice smothered in oyster sauce. Poor Bartlett couldn't get enough and shoveled it into his mouth first with the fork and then with the spoon.

The kitchen door blew open and Su Li padded into the room with tiny steps from her oversized feet. Black hair piled high, face powered white, lips bright red and smiling; she looked exactly like a Chinese porcelain doll, so fetching that I almost didn't notice the roast goose sizzling tantalizingly from the tray she carried.

To my great surprise Bartlett didn't notice the goose

either. Instead the big lug leaped to his feet so fast his chair flew halfway across the barroom. He ripped his beat up black hat from the rat's nest atop his head and stood there with his jaw scraping the floor, staring at Su Li as if he'd seen a ghost, and holding the hat over his privates like a man caught with his pants down.

Su Li must have been scared out of her lily white rice powdered skin by the sight of such an ugly awkward ogre looming over her looking about as stupid as he really was. The tray with the roast goose began to teeter and would have toppled to the floor had Rafael not had the good sense to grab it and put it safely on the table.

I was sure that all my good intentions were to go up in smoke. Clearly terrified at the pathetic creature standing before her and fully aware of our plan to have her marry the poor rube as a way to escape her life at the cathouse, Su Li would no doubt turn and bolt for the door as soon as she recovered her senses.

Then, to my utter amazement, she cracked a small smile, stuck her hands together inside the spacious sleeves of her quilted bathrobe, bowed low in front of Bartlett and said something so soft and sweet in Chinese that even a hard nosed former three-card monte dealer like me had to sniffle back a tear or two. She looked up at the big dope and blessed him with a smile so warm it would have melted all the snow at the top of the highest mountain in the Sierra Nevada.

Suddenly it dawned on me that Su Li just might actually like Bartlett. Why I couldn't fathom but what man can comprehend the wilds of a woman's mind. "Bartlett," I cried. "She's the one. I found her for you. Don't be a coward. Ask her to marry you before she changes her mind."

His head swung toward me, eyes wild. "Me, marry her?" he asked in a trembling voice.

"Yeah, you!" I yelled. "Ask her quick before it's too late."

A weird, lopsided smile crept across his kisser, his wide eyes rolled dreamily around his head. "Yeah," he whispered mostly to himself as he dropped to his knees and took the poor girl's teensy hand in his gigantic paw just as gently as a mother would when powdering her baby's bottom. "Will you marry me?" he mumbled, looking for all the world like a man who'd had too much punch at a Saturday night dance.

Her ruby red lips beamed back at him as her alabaster face bobbed up and down in answer. I, for one, stood totally stunned that such a beautiful, fragile thing could ever agree to enter into holy matrimony with a galoot as homely as Bottomless Bartlett.

"Bartlett," I yelled. "My two hundred dollars!"

He never took his eyes from her, just reached into his pocket, pulled out a leather bag and tossed it in my direction. Luckily I managed to snag it before it crashed into the cut glass mirror behind the bar. Then he swept her into his arms like a man does when he carries his new bride over the threshold and headed for the door.

"Where you going, Bartlett?" I yelled.

"Find a preacher," he said, his eyes still glued on Su Li.

"But its storming like blue blazes out there," I reminded him.

"Yeah," he said, then ducked out the door with Su Li still in his arms and disappeared into the muddy mess of Clay Street.

The kitchen door banged open and Jasper strode up to the bar and held out his hand. "I be takin' Ah Hoi's hundred dollars an' da' rye whiskey ya owes me, Willie."

I popped a new bottle of Buzzards Breath Rye onto the bar and pushed the leather pouch over to him. "Split it up yourself, Jasper. Ah Hoi don't trust me no how," I mumbled, still stunned that a fellow like Bottomless Bartlett could win himself such a beautiful bride so easy. It made me think there just might be a slim chance for an old rotten-hearted barkeep like me.

"Señor, what do we do with the goose?" Rafael asked, a carving knife in hand.

I looked up. That goose sure smelled inviting. "Ain't no use to let Su Li's good cooking go to waste." I said.

"Su Li?" Jasper blurted. "Why dat gal cain't boil water what she don't burn some. All dis stuff fixed up by Miss Ah Hoi's private cook, Wang Chow."

"Wang Chow," I mutter. "You mean –"

"Yessah, Mistah Willie. She cain't cook a lick."

"Oh Lord! Next you'll tell me Su Li talks English." I said, sure that was a total impossibility.

"Oh, yessah. She yammers away at all dah customers 'bout mendin' they sinning ways. Miss Ah Hoi so mad at her she made her cook, just to keep her out da way."

"You mean –"

"Yessah, Mistah Willie. Ya done been had again. Dat gal went to a Mission School in China. Cain't cook a'tall but she talks bettah'n I does."

"Well, I'll be a monkey's uncle. What about poor Bartlett?" I moan.

"Oh, Señor Bartlett will be fine, I think," Rafael opined then sliced off a healthy chunk of goose and popped it into his mouth.

"Yeah! After all he's the one that got the gal." I pulled out another bottle of Buzzards Breath and filled three glasses on the bar. "Bring that bird over here, Rafael. We may as well celebrate. Our good friend Bartlett is getting married today." I raise my glass in a toast. "Here's to Bottomless Bartlett and his beautiful bride," I proclaimed.

"Si, si," cried Rafael

"Yessah, Mistah Willie," Jasper agreed.

"Drink up and dig into the goose, friends. I reckon we've seen the last of those two for a while."

And truer words were rarely spoken. Right after the honeymoon Bartlett shelled out the lion's share of the gold he'd mined for a restaurant along the waterfront. But with Su Li's warm smile to greet the customers and Bartlett's brand new brother-in-law Wang Chow cooking, the place straightaway became the tastiest and most popular eatery around. It just goes to show ya. You never can tell about folks these days.

The End

Ellen Gray Massey –

Ellen Gray Massey, born at Nevada, Missouri, has lived in Laclede County since 1946 and taught for forty-two years: at Conway Elementary, and Hartville and Lebanon High Schools, and on adjunct faculty for Drury University's Graduate Education program. She now teaches Elderhostel classes for the YMCA of the Ozarks at Potosi, and for Ozark Adventures, Inc. in Branson. A speaker and writer, she promotes the Ozarks. Since 1990 she has given over 360 talks about the Ozarks and about writing. She was a teacher/advisor from 1973-1983 of *Bittersweet, the Ozark Quarterly*, published by her students at Lebanon High School and has done other editorial work professionally and for friends. She has published numerous articles, short stories, essays, a musical play, as well as 15 novels and 8 non-fiction books. In 1995 she was inducted into the first Writers Hall of Fame of America. She has won 24 awards from the Missouri Writers Guild and three times finalist in Western Writers of America's Golden Spur Awards.

Her recent non-fiction books are *Family Fun and Games, The Bittersweet Ozarks at a Glance*, and editor of *Mysteries of the Ozarks, Vol. I, II,. III, and IV.* Her recent novels *New Hope* and *The Burnt District* were published by Hard Shell Word Factory, an online and print publisher, and *Brothers, Blue and Gray* and *Her Enemies, Blue and Gray* and *Morning in Nicodemus* by Goldminds Publishing.

Her web site is www.ellengraymassey.com

FREEDOM FORD

Ellen Gray Massey

As Walking Owl paddled around the bend in the icy Osage River, he was surprised to see a woman wrapped in a faded comforter fishing from the river bank.

Quietly, the Osage nosed his canoe into the soft mud bank and stabbed his paddle into the river bottom to arrest his movement. He did not want to startle her by his sudden appearance.

Back on one of his infrequent trapping trips to the Blue Mounds area to visit his ancestral grounds near the grave of his grandfather, he was traveling upstream to check his catch.

So that the woman would not think he was an outlaw or a Jayhawker, he shed his wool coat and felt hat and searched through his knapsack for his Osage headband and leather jerkin. He reasoned she would not be afraid of an Indian as White-Osage relations in this area had always been amicable; the Osages had peacefully moved to Kansas and only occasionally returned to trap. He had been careful this trip to avoid notice because of the troubles between the Missourians and the Kansas Jayhawkers over whether Kansas would enter the Union as a free or slave state. Preacher Jim

Anderson and John Brown often raided these western border counties of Missouri to kidnap slaves and take them back to Kansas. Encouraged by the growing hostility and unrest, other men used slavery as an excuse to raid, rape, and kill.

The borderland in 1858 was not a safe place for anyone, let alone Indians and Blacks.

As he purposely rattled the steel traps in his canoe, Walking Owl paddled around the bend in full sight. The woman jerked up, stumbled in the folds of the comforter, and dropped her pole.

"Don't be alarmed," Walking Owl's soft voice came from the opposite side of the river. His English was perfect. "I am Walking Owl of the Osages on a trapping trip. I met Caleb Watson here two years ago and he gave me permission to trap." The woman's rigid pose relaxed as soon as she heard his cultured voice. "Are you Watson's wife?" he asked.

"Yes." She expelled her pent up breath. "I'm Etta Watson. Caleb spoke about you."

Walking Owl remembered that Watson had just built his house and with the help of his two slaves had broken some of the prairie sod on his farm. He knew the richness of the area. His people had lived for generations on this borderland of the eastern hardwood forests and the western prairie. He was a child when his chief moved the tribe to Kansas.

He remembered something else from his casual meeting two years ago. Watson was letting his slaves pay for their freedom by their labor. The couple should be free by now.

A bite on the line pulled Etta's pole down the mud bank. She grabbed too late. The pole hit the water and, tugged by the fish, started down the river. With dexterous strokes from his paddle, Walking Owl retrieved the pole. In seconds, a bass flopped on a pile of pelts in the canoe. He beached in an inlet downstream from Etta and handed her the fish as he rose to his full six feet ten inches.

Both of them laughed. Etta's eyes sparkled at sight of the four pound fish.

Their pleasure was cut short when they heard two rifle shots from the Watson house.

"Caleb and the children!" Etta cried. She saw smoke coming from within a cabin near the barn, "They're after Ned and Tillie!"

She dropped her fish and comforter and raced through the marshy lowland onto the field of corn stubble. Walking Owl sprinted after her, cut in front of her, and forced her out of the open field into the trees. They crouched together hidden behind an oak trunk.

From near the smoking cabin came repeated piercing female cries. At Walking Owl's questioning look, Etta whispered, "Tillie."

"Your slave?"

Etta nodded and then moaned, "She and Ned are free now."

Walking Owl counted two mounted men with rifles who circled the big house; they yelled as they made a game of dodging the sporadic shotgun blasts from the house. In front of the smoking cabin a bearded man on foot stood guard over a middle-aged Black couple. The outlaw's bay horse, tethered to a post of the empty corral, pranced around afraid of the fire. White smoke poured from the open door of the cabin. Fingers of orange fire flickered across the back window. Suddenly the whole cabin was in flames.

"Jayhawkers are burning Ned's house," Etta cried. "And

the barn."

"Any horses?" Walking Owl asked as he remembered that Watson owned several horses and a substantial herd of cattle.

"All stolen!" Her teary eyes looked at Walking Owl. "Nothing left to steal. Except Tillie and Ned."

"I'll swing around and try to reach them," Walking Owl said. She nodded. He handed her a Smith and Wesson pistol. When she smiled her appreciation and gently ran her finger over the cold metal, he knew she was familiar with guns. "At the main house, will your husband keep the two men busy?"

"Yes. I'll get behind the shed to pin them in Caleb's cross-fire." At Walking Owl's surprised look, she continued. "We've had other attacks. We know what to do. Jeremy and the little girls, they help."

The two parted. With the barn blocking him from the outlaws' sight, Walking Owl ran noiselessly through the corn stubble, skirted the barn, and squatted behind a wood pile. Downwind from the fire and partially hidden in the smoke, he was within range of the man holding Ned and Tillie. He pulled his kerchief over his nose and waited for Etta to get into position.

Tillie's screams subsided; Ned's deep voice tried to calm her. They were bound back to back to prevent their escape. Tillie's dress was torn at her waist. Mud covered Ned's shirt and trousers; blood dripped from a cut on his cheek. When Ned and Tillie tried to side-step away, the bearded captor struck them with the butt of his gun.

"Ain't ya had enough?" the outlaw asked, his attention distracted by the commotion at the house.

"Yee-e-e-hi-i-i!" the black-coated attacker yelled. He shot

at the house as he circled it.

Ignoring the blood on his face, Ned struggled to loosen the ropes while the bearded man watched his partners. "Stupid fool," the captor said as he struck Ned again, "cain't ya see we're freein' ya?"

"We're already free," Ned cried. "We own land here."

"Yeah," the bearded man sneered, "and I'm president of the bank." He shoved Ned so hard that he fell, dragging Tillie with him.

Lying on the ground, hands tied and unable to get up, Ned used his feet. When the outlaw leaned over, with the barrel of his gun in the air ready to strike again, Ned kicked him in the groin.

In agony and holding himself with one hand, the outlaw swore as he hopped around doubled over. Ned and Tillie worked together to stand up. Just as they were erect and side-stepping to escape into the smoke screen, the bearded man shot above their heads and at the ground at their feet. One bullet struck Ned's leg. Ned looked in disbelief at the hole in his trouser leg and the redness that oozed out.

"Don't ya move," the outlaw hissed, "or I'll shoot yer damn black feet clean off."

The couple froze.

In position by the shed, Etta signaled to Walking Owl. They each fired at the two men who circled the house. The shots from inside the house increased.

"Let's git the hell outta here," the black-coated leader yelled. He galloped his roan toward the bearded man. "Git them two and let's ride."

His stout partner fired a parting shot at the house and followed. He jumped out of the saddle and cut the ropes that bound the couple together, and while the bearded man wrestled with Ned, he grabbed Tillie around her waist. He ignored her blows and kicks as he tossed her like a sack of meal on his horse and remounted.

Walking Owl stepped into the open, his tall figure materializing out of the smoke. When he saw the Osage, the bearded man gasped and abandoned Ned. He vaulted on his gelding and mercilessly spurred after his two partners.

Ned struggled out of his bonds and stood up just as Walking Owl reached him. With a powerful lunge in spite of his leg wound, Ned tackled the Osage.

"Hold on, friend," Walking Owl said, "Save your strength to get your wife back."

Ned noticed the Osage's headband and jerkin, and calmed by his voice, he paused long enough for Walking Owl to grab his hands and explain who he was.

"Well, come on," Ned cried, and then jumped up and limped down the road after the vanishing outlaws. "Tillie!" he screamed.

Walking Owl blocked his way. "Easy, friend. We'll get her back. Better have a plan first."

A young boy and two smaller girls burst out of the house into Etta's arms. Ill and weak, Caleb Watson steadied himself against the door jam while he still held a twelve gauge shotgun. "We're not hurt," he said as Etta ran to him. Her children hung on to her, all three talking through their tears as they re-entered the warm house.

"Papa made us hide under the bed," one of the girls said. Supported by his wife, Caleb turned to the Osage. "Walking Owl, welcome." The two men shook hands. "We are grateful."

"They took Tillie!" Jeremy cried, as he looked at the four adults in turn.

No one answered him. Trying to hide a cough, Caleb fell weakly into his chair. Etta examined Ned's leg wound.

"Just nicked you," she said. "Didn't hit the bone, but you've lost some blood. Need to stay off of it."

"Can't," Ned said. With much difficulty he stood erect even though he swayed slightly. "Gotta git Tillie."

"Mrs. Watson is right," Walking Owl said. He stepped up to the doorway. "I'll go after Tillie while she dresses your leg."

Both Ned and Etta shook their heads. "I'm going with you," Etta said to Walking Owl. All three men objected. "Yes, I'm the one to go. Walking Owl needs help against three men. And Ned, we need you here in the house in case the outlaws come back." When his pain made Ned sit down, she turned back to the Osage. "Caleb can doctor Ned's leg better'n I can."

Walking Owl studied the determined woman. She had demonstrated her quickness and skill with a gun. "You're right," he said. "Everyone can help. Jeremy, you run to the river and get the bass your mother caught. Girls, get the stove going to fry it. I don't figure you've eaten in a while. Caleb and Ned can watch the road in case the outlaws return."

"They won't return today," Caleb said. "Nothing left here for them. They came for Ned and Tillie. They'll have to take Tillie to their camp first." A spell of coughing doubled him over.

Ned groaned and again tried to stand up.

"What'll they do to Tillie?" Jeremy cried.

"Nothing," Walking Owl said, "because I'll get her back." Then he asked Caleb, "They didn't come here to free the slaves?"

Both Caleb and Ned shook their heads. "No," Ned said. "They'll steal anything that'll bring 'em money. The burnin' and killin' is jest for fun."

"So they won't take Tillie to Kansas?" Walking Owl asked.

"No," Caleb said. "They'll take her to Independence to sell at the slave auction after they – "

Ned groaned and slumped into his chair with his head in his hands.

Etta disappeared into a back room. Still wearing her stocking cap, she returned dressed in her husband's coat and trousers, with Walking Owl's pistol thrust in her belt. "We're wasting time," she said.

Walking Owl nodded. "They'll have to cross the river?"

Caleb nodded. "At Freedom Ford."

Walking Owl did not remember a ford of that name.

"Tillie named it that," Ned said, "when Caleb brought us here a few years ago and promised us our freedom."

"Good name. Could we beat them there if we paddled up the river?"

"If we hurry," Etta said. "The road swings back east for a few miles and is crooked and rough all the way."

"They won't hurry since we don't have any horses to chase after them," Caleb said.

"We'll get Tillie back," Walking Owl assured Ned. "You stay and protect the family." He did not wait to hear Ned's agreement, but disappeared out the door, tailed by Etta.

By the time Etta reached the river, Walking Owl had removed his trapping gear and pelts and was ready to push off. He put on his wool coat and felt hat. He folded Etta's old comforter and laid it on his knapsack. She pushed the canoe to dislodge it from the bank, jumped into the front, and grabbed the extra paddle.

Walking Owl avoided the strong current in the center of the river. He paddled the canoe the three miles to the ford. When possible, he stayed under the bluff for added cover in case the outlaws would spot them.

Silently the canoe moved upstream. Tillie's periodic screams reached them when the twisty trail on the bluff came close to the river.

"She's letting us know where they are," Etta said.

Walking Owl nodded agreement, his body tense from listening to all the sounds. Over the soft lapping of the water against the canoe and the almost imperceptible gurgle of the water as the paddles cut into it, he distinguished the voices of the men. He caught a few words before the trail veered away from the river.

"You said they was only one sick man there," came the words of one of the men.

"Where'd that there giant come from?"

"Sell her in Independence." This was followed by Tillie's screams.

Walking Owl paddled with powerful strokes. In the quieter water along the banks, he avoided logs, overhanging branches, and the icy rim along the bank while his eyes missed nothing. He listened for sounds to judge the outlaws' location and speed. Caleb had surmised correctly. The men were in no hurry. Tillie's screams and the outlaws' voices, along with the horses' hoof beats, told him that he and Etta would reach the ford before them.

Etta's back was rigid as she held the paddle in her mittened hands. Neither said anything though she occasionally turned to look at Walking Owl. He smiled encouragement and nodded approval. "I won't let them harm Tillie," the position of his body seemed to say. Gradually, Etta relaxed.

Walking Owl recognized the ford ahead, a shallower channel where the water ran over a rocky shelf-like outcrop. He paddled to the western bank to a tree-covered cove. He backed in, breaking the thin ice coating on the still water. Holding to overhanging limbs, he stepped onto solid ground, and pulled the canoe up the bank to steady it for Etta to step out. In the twenty-five degree weather they were careful to keep dry.

"The man that has Tillie is in the middle," Walking Owl whispered. "They'll cross the river in that order, one at a time." He pointed across the river where the men would soon appear. "After the black-coated man crosses and goes on down the road, there," he pointed behind him where the road continued in its northwesterly direction through the trees, "when he gets across, can you deal with him?"

Etta held up Walking Owl's pistol for answer.

The Osage heard the horses approaching through the trees across the river and motioned for her to follow him. They hurried the two hundred feet upstream through the under-brush, as they dodged the trees and avoided the swampy regions to Freedom Ford. They crouched behind a huge oak where the trail emerged out of the river. Across the stream the road entered an easy slope down to the rocky ford.

When the outlaws appeared, their horses stepped cautiously onto the rocky approach. Walking Owl whispered, "When the second man with Tillie crosses the river, I'll cut her free and take care of him and the third fellow."

Walking Owl cocked his head toward the west to tell Etta it was time for her to get into position. He clasped her hand in encouragement. Both crept out of sight.

Following the black-coated leader came the stout outlaw with Tillie tied behind him. The rope that bound her hands together was fastened loosely around his waist. She sat upright, alert for any opportunity to escape. Her body trembled with the cold. Last came the bearded man, who muttered while he slumped in his saddle, his head down.

The leader did not see the Osage on the side of the trail behind a sycamore tree. Nor did he notice on the other side of the trail Etta's brown coat or her black wool stocking cap that protruded above a fallen log.

The bearded man continued to grumble.

"Shet up," the stout man said. "It's yer fault. Easy, ya said. Jest one sick man."

"Well, it was when I freed his hosses and cattle and all his grub." He laughed at his own wit. "I didn't figure on the slaves fightin' us."

"And ya didn't figure on two more guns," the leader said. "Ya 'most got us killed."

"Where'd they come from?" the stout man asked.

"From outta the smoke." The bearded one looked around nervously. "I seen a giant ghost."

"Ever heerd a ghost shootin' a gun?" The leader laughed.

"It come floatin' outta the burnin' barn, rollin' along the ground with the smoke. Then it stood up. Eight, nine feet tall. I seen it."

While the men were distracted, Tillie worked at the cords around her wrists. When her captor pulled tighter on the rope connecting them, she cried out at in pain. "Cheer up," he said to the bearded man, "We done good. Giant ghost or not, this 'ere gal'll bring five, six hundred." He grinned and patted Tillie. Since Tillie could not kick him, she spat at him. As he ducked, the outlaw laughed. "Freed 'em from their owners," He laughed and patted Tillie again. "Then we sell 'em."

"And we git the money." The bearded one began to cheer up.

"So quit yer grumblin'. If you wasn't so clumsy, we'd have the big buck, too."

The outlaws failed to distinguish among the natural river sounds a soft "Bob, bob white," and, after a pause, another call. They were so preoccupied with their greed that they did not spot a black stocking cap that waved above a rotting moss-covered log.

Walking Owl did not miss either sign. Nor did he miss Tillie's actions. She looked quickly in Etta's direction, jerked herself upright in her seat behind the outlaw, and increased her struggles.

The leader urged his roan into the cold water. When he reached the western side, he spurred his horse to make him leap up the mud bank. From the top, he waved the others on. Then he spurred his roan on down the trail.

The stout man's big mare stepped gingerly into the water. More slowly than the leader's roan because of her double load, the mare carefully placed each hoof down on the slick rocky bottom as the current swirled around her legs.

The stout man had difficulty encouraging the mare and holding his seat while Tillie constantly fought him. The mare slipped several times, going down to her knees once.

The diversion was what Walking Owl needed. With his rifle slung across his back, and his knife unsheathed, he waited. The mare reached the mud bank, paused, and then scrambled up the slippery bank with her two riders. Tillie lunged against the outlaw's back with the whole force of her body. He jerked the reins; the mare slipped back.

Walking Owl leaped. He landed between Tillie and the outlaw. His force knocked mare and riders to the ground. At the same time two pistol shots rang out in the woods west of him.

With his boot heel dug into the mud bank for anchorage, Walking Owl grabbed Tillie's arm and quickly cut the ropes. Caught unaware, Tillie started to struggle, until she recognized him as the one who rescued Ned. Freed, she grabbed a tree root. The mare quickly righted herself, jumped the bank, and galloped upstream through the trees.

The enraged outlaw rolled over. He kicked Walking Owl's legs out from under him. Both men struggled as they slid and rolled down the bank. When they reached the water line, the outlaw was on the bottom. As he splashed into the cold water, he called out in pain, giving the Osage the advantage. Walking Owl jumped back; his boots sunk several inches into the icy mud along the water's edge. His powerful shove pushed the stout man farther into the river. He sunk out of sight for a few seconds before emerging with a gasp that turned into curses.

Tillie pulled herself to level ground and disappeared behind some logs and bushes. With Tillie safe for the moment, and the stout man temporarily out of action – his horse gone and his gun wet and useless – Walking Owl had only the bearded man across the river to contend with.

In action now after his initial surprise when the Osage dropped from the sky, the third outlaw had pulled his rifle from its case and took aim. Walking Owl leaped to level ground. He rose to his full height as he reached over his shoulder for his rifle and leaped behind an oak just as the bearded man's first shot struck the bank. There was no second shot. Still seated on his gelding, a perfect target for Walking Owl, the outlaw seemed frozen in fear of the tall Osage.

Walking Owl fired at the ground in front of the horse. The gelding reared. The bearded man hit the ground; his gun flew from his hands and slid over the rocky surface. Snorting and bucking, the horse fled back down the road he had just traveled. Swearing loudly, the outlaw scrambled for his rifle. Walking Owl's next shot struck the gun. It bounced a few inches into the air and slid over the wet rocks closer to the river.

With his peripheral vision Walking Owl saw the stout man wading toward the bank. The Osage sent a shot in his direction, not at the man, but between him and the bank to force him to stay in the river. After a few minutes in the icy water, he would be no threat for a long time.

The Osage melted into the trees. The stout man muttered curses as he pulled himself out of the water. On foot with wet and damaged guns, the two outlaws were harmless for the present.

But the leader . . . ?

Since the two pistol shots, he had heard nothing from Etta, nor from Tillie after she climbed the river bank. He heard the hoof beats of the bearded man's fleeing gelding. He cocked his head upstream to listen and thought he recognized the movement of the stout man's mare through the trees.

But there was no sound from Etta's direction. He hesitated, debating whether to go down the road to see about her and the black-coated leader, or . . . .

A call of a bobwhite came from the direction of his canoe. Reassured, Walking Owl sprinted downstream. In the hidden cove, the two women were seated in his canoe, Etta at the bow, Tillie bent over in the middle wrapped in the comforter.

"We're all right," Etta whispered in answer to his unspoken question as he glanced at both women. Though Tillie's short hair and face was plastered with mud from the roll on the mud bank, the only change in Etta was that her stocking cap had been pulled on carelessly.

Walking Owl climbed into his seat. He thrust his paddle against a tree root and gave a powerful push. Silently the long canoe glided into the current.

A pistol shot knocked Walking Owl's hat from his head into the canoe. Another shot splintered the back of the canoe above the water line. Tillie gave a muffled scream and fell forward to lie in the bottom of the boat. Walking Owl glimpsed the figure of a man on the bluff behind him. He was too far away to distinguish which outlaw it was. Walking Owl and Etta leaned over to avoid the bullets and paddled rapidly to get out of pistol range. A third and fourth shot splatted harmlessly behind them.

When out of range of the sniper, Walking Owl asked Etta, "Was that your man, the black-coat?"

"No." Her voice and the stiffness of her body left no doubt.

"Then the bearded man had a pistol."

As he continued to paddle rapidly, and taking advantage

of the current in the center of the river, Walking Owl seemed to make the canoe fly through the water. Tillie sobbed softly. Her shoulders shook; her whole body trembled.

"We're safe now, Tillie," Etta said. Though she did not cease her paddling, she turned to look at her friend several times to give her encouragement. "This is Walking Owl."

Tillie twisted her upper body to face him. "Thank you," she said in a voice hoarse from her screams. Walking Owl inclined his head in response and handed her a blanket from his knapsack; his eyes searched the bluffs for the outlaw. She wrapped the blanket around her, leaving only her face exposed.

When Tillie's tremors stopped, Walking Owl asked gently, "Did the men harm you?"

"No." She studied this tall man who had stepped out of the smoke to save Ned at the farm and dropped from the sky to rescue her at Freedom Ford. "You really are a giant. One of the outlaws thought you was a ghost. He was too scared to shoot straight when he seen you back there at the ford."

"I was counting on that."

They continued rapidly. Though uneasy about the outlaws attacking them on the river, Walking Owl was more worried about the people at the Watson house. If the bearded man caught up to them so quickly on the river, it was possible he might return to the house. And he was concerned about Tillie's long exposure without a coat. His toes were beginning to stiffen where his boots had leaked. Etta missed a few strokes in her paddling to blow on her hands to warm them up. They must reach the house quickly.

He had miscalculated back at the ford. He figured they would be safe from pursuit at least until the stout outlaw built a fire to dry his clothes and until both outlaws could catch their horses. He should have killed both of them, but to avoid any possible repercussions against his tribe, he never shot to kill White men, even outlaws.

Tillie examined Walking Owl, from his muddy, leather boots up his long, lean body to the hole in his hat, which once again was on his head. When she caught his black eyes looking at her from under his wide hat brim, she asked, "Where'd you come from?"

Walking Owl grinned for the first time; crinkly lines appeared around his eyes. "Actually, just a few miles from here." He swung his arm to the east. "Blue Mounds." When Tillie opened her mouth in disbelief, he added. "That was a long time ago. I'm from Kansas back on a trapping trip."

"Oh." Tillie wrapped Walking Owl's wool blanket tighter around her. "Why'd you leave here?" she asked.

"My grandfather moved us to our Kansas lands. It was the only way for us to survive."

"It's crazy," Tillie said. "White men got your people off of this land and then brought us coloreds in. And now they want us out too. Don't make sense."

"Caleb and I want you here, and we want Walking Owl, too," Etta said.

Tillie looked back at Walking Owl's immobile face. "I didn't want to come here in the first place, but now I don't want to leave."

"I didn't want to leave." The women had to strain to hear Walking Owl's words. "I'm trying to find a way to return."

Tillie shook her head sadly. "You can't return. And Ned and I must leave." Walking Owl nodded as they turned the last bend of the river before reaching Watson land.

"No, Tillie," Etta said. "You don't have to leave. This trouble will soon be over."

"Tillie is right." Walking Owl said. "What's happening on this border is just the beginning."

"But, Walking Owl, you can pass for a White man."

"But Ned and I can't," Tillie said. "Though we're no longer slaves, we still ain't free."

After a careful search of the area for hidden men, Walking Owl directed the canoe into the Watson cove. "No one in this borderland is free, Tillie, not you and Ned, not me, or the Watsons."

Etta tied the canoe to an exposed root. "It'll be better one day, and Freedom Ford will represent what you named it for, Tillie."

As Tillie extricated herself from the folds of the blanket, she looked at Walking Owl and shook her head sadly.

All was quiet at the homestead. Smoke curled from the chimney. As they crossed the corn field, Tillie repressed a sob at the sight of the pile of embers that was her home. "The outlaws will be back," Tillie said.

"Probably," Walking Owl agreed.

"But not right away," Etta said. "We won't let them harm you."

Tillie shook her head. "Can't live like this. Gotta leave. They'll be back, or others will."

When they were halfway across the field, Jeremy and his sisters burst out of the house, running toward them. This time they crowded around Tillie; they hugged and kissed her.

"The fish is ready," Jeremy said to Walking Owl. "Papa ate some and feels better. He doctored Ned's leg. It's gonna get well." As proof he pointed to the doorstep where Caleb and

Ned stood.

Though assured by the men that there was no sign of outlaws, Walking Owl was worried about the one with the pistol. He excused himself to scout out the trail.

"They are gone," he said when he returned. "The tracks say that the bearded man caught his bay and crossed the river. There's nobody on this side. Keep a constant lookout for them. Now I must return to Kansas."

He shook hands with Caleb and the children. As he turned to Ned and Tillie, he asked, "You'll come to me when you get to Kansas?" They both nodded. "Don't wait too long."

When he reached Etta he looked into her eyes for a few seconds. "You didn't tell us what happened to the black-coated outlaw on the roan."

"No."

Caleb took her hand. "Do you want to tell us?"

She looked long into her husband's fever-bright eyes. She glanced at young Jeremy and at her two little daughters. She looked at her undamaged house and to their rich prairie acres behind the still-glowing ashes of the barn. She glanced over the sooty blotch on the land where once stood Ned and Etta's cabin. Then her eyes settled on Ned. A scab was already forming on the cut on his handsome face. His bandaged leg was propped up on a footstool, and his torn shirt exposed his bruised arm. His right hand covered Tillie's hand on his shoulder. Tillie stood behind him, her dress stained with mud from the ford.

Etta then turned back to Walking Owl. "My dear friend, today you saved the lives of everybody here. All you asked me to do was to 'deal with the man on the roan'."

"And . . . ?"

"I dealt with him." She handed Walking Owl his pistol.

Walking Owl held up his hand in an Osage farewell. When Jeremy and his sisters crowded to the window to wave good-bye, he was not in sight.

The End

Pamela Foster –

Pamela Foster is an award-winning author whose mainstream novel, *Redneck Goddess,* was published in July of 2011 and whose short stories have been published in the anthology of the Ozarks Writers League, Voices, as well in Frontier Tales. Two more novels, *Bigfoot Blues* and *Noisy Creek* will be released in 2012. She's an addicted attendee at the weekly meetings of the critique group, Northwest Arkansas Writers Workshop, and is a member of Ozark Writers League, Oklahoma Writers Federation and Ozark Creative Writers. She writes every morning and loves to hear from fans.

www.authorpamelafoster.com
pamelafoster2011@gmail.com

OZARK CHILD

Pamela Foster

The air carries the first soft hint of spring, warmer than past mornings with a promise of awakening red dirt. I scramble out from under the Double Four Patch quilt my mama sewed specially for me from calico sacks as soft against my skin as the white flour they held. The pine boards are cold on my bare feet as I pad to the window. When I was little, this here window was bigger than my whole head and I could stand flat-footed and look out onto the hills that are the silent guardians of our life.

In spring and summer my morning greeting is thick green, each fall my view is speckled with oranges and yellows, and in winter I see black trees that reach their naked branches to heaven as though they're praying to God for an end to the infernal cold. This morning I hike up my nightgown so as not to get it dirty before kneeling and pressing my face against the cold glass.

The mud puddles in the yard shimmer like old silver mama packed with her all the way from Illinois when she and my daddy came here nine years ago. Beauregard is already in

207

the field behind the barn, his black nose to the ground, his stubby tail aiming for the sky. I can hear my daddy on the front porch stomping his boots on the bottom step. The milking done, he's coming in to breakfast.

I pull my nightgown over my head quick as I can but the cold air still tickles my skin with goose bumps before I can pull on my last year's Christmas present (I pretended it was a surprise even though I watched my mama knit that green sweater for practically every night the whole month of November). Mama says next year, when I turn ten, I have to start wearing dresses, but with one more year of freedom promised me, I step into the overalls mama cut down from daddy's after he wore them plumb out at the knees and seat.

I am itching to get outside with Beau but I know any exploring will have to wait until after breakfast and chores. I climb down the stairs barefoot, knowing my boots and socks are waiting warm as toast beside the wood stove where mama is just now lifting a flapjack from the cast iron fry pan to my plate.

By the time I've helped clear the breakfast dishes, swept the front porch, and filled the kindling box, the sun has melted the silver puddles into ordinary red slush. Mama is kneading bread for dinner when I reach inside the front door, snatch my jacket from its hook and wave to let her know I'm headed for the woods. She flutters a floury hand of dismissal at me. Beau and I don't wait for her to think of any more chores. We make our escape across the hard packed dirt of the yard.

Daddy is stringing fence. I stop a while and watch a flock of young crows as they make themselves a torment to him. The shiny black birds squawk and caw and fly in a disorganized circle just over his head. Then, as though encouraged by an audience, a few of the birds begin dropping like rocks from the sky, pulling up in a sharp arch inches from his head. When Daddy removes his wide brimmed hat and waves it in the air, they leave off that fun and begin swooping down, stealing the shiny hog rings he's using on the fencing.

"If you're gonna stand around and encourage the devils, you may as well help me with this here fencing."

I press my mouth into a trembling line to stop the laughing and Beau and I take ourselves down to the creek.

Deep in a pile of musky leaf litter, I find a brown and orange salamander. Just about the time I'm done fooling with that creature, Beau discovers a black millipede wiggling its way over a pale green patch of moss. After that I skin both elbows and one knee stealing an empty sparrow's nest from the branches of the sweetgum tree that angles itself out over the summer swimming hole. With the nest secured in the bib pocket of my overalls, Beau locates a lumpy hop toad which we imprison for a while in a cage of creek stones.

My belly is beginning to rub up against my backbone and this is generally a clear sign that my mama is going to be wanting help with putting dinner on the table. Then Beau is tearing hell bent for leather, his nose to the ground headed up the rocky bank that marks the border of our land. By the time I scramble up the embankment, Beau is digging frantically at the roots of a scaly-bark hickory unearthing what looks like a small den. It's not that I don't know better than to stick my head into the home of a wild animal. I even hear a still small voice, that sounds remarkably like my mama's, shouting for me to step back. But Beau is digging like a fiend, leaf mold and black dirt is flying and I simply cannot stop myself from pulling the slobber-faced dog away and squeezing my face into that hole to see what we've found.

I'm looking into the round face of a baby badger. There is a scream. I can't say with certainty whether this squeal came from me or the badger, both of us being about equally surprised. Without his mama for protection this tiny creature hesitates not one instant before he lunges, connecting one knife-sharp front claw with my surprised face. When I jerk my bloody chin out of that hole, Beau rushes in.

"I bet we could tame him down. Keep him for a pet," I tell the dog, who lifts his own torn face from the ground, cocks his head to the side, looks at me like I've lost what little sense I possessed at the beginning of this day.

It's not like I don't know that messing further with this formidable creature is what my mama would call, 'a failure of reason.' But with both Beau and me running blood, our dander is up and there ain't no way we're backing away from this here challenge.

Between the two of us we manage to get just under a pound of soft fur, ripping claws and evil teeth up out of that den. The badger is making a shrieking racket that brings to mind the crying and gnashing of teeth that Preacher is fond of describing. I take off my jacket, drop it over soft fur, slashing claws, and snapping teeth. Then, with a growling ball of badger pressed tight, flattening that bird's nest against my chest, Beau and I use the cawing of young crows as a beacon and we pump our legs as fast as we can to get our prize to Daddy.

It takes a buckboard ride into Fayetteville and twenty-one stitches to put me and Beau to rights again. The dog got the worst of it with sixteen. His left ear hangs a little crooked but I believe it gives him a jaunty look. My chin is sore from my own meeting with Doctor Swanson. I swear the sewing hurt a heap more than the original damage done by the baby badger. Worst of all was my daddy's scolding and my mama's crying nearly the entirety of the hour long trip to town.

Right now Beau has been given special permission to sleep on my bed and the two of us are tucked in snug under the soft quilt. Daddy made me a promise that he would return the badger to its den, but he told it to me in the exact same voice he used last Christmas Eve to convince me to go to sleep so as Santa could come. Mama has declared that starting tomorrow I will be wearing a dress every day of the dang week and that I'll be doing my exploring within sight of the front porch for a goodly long time.

I rub Beau's right ear gently between my thumb and pointy finger, kiss the top of his whiskered face, fall into a dream of unruly crows, warm flapjacks, and the discoveries to be made under nearly every mossy rock and rotten log in Northwest Arkansas.

The End

Nancy Hartney –

Nancy Hartney contributes articles and photographs to *The Chronicle of the Horse, Sidelines,* and the *Horsemen's Roundup.* Her book reviews have appeared in the *Fort Worth Star Telegram,* general motorcycle touring articles with photographs in *American Iron,* and community interest pieces in the *Northwest Arkansas Times.* While continuing to write non-fiction, she has turned her pen to fiction with short stories appearing in *Voices, Echoes of the Ozarks, and Cactus Country.* She lives in Fayetteville, Arkansas.

THE WHITE OAK'S TALE

Nancy Hartney

The white oak tree had grown on a sweet grass knoll at the edge of the plains for more than a hundred years. It stood against endless wind, grew great and unbending through drought-brown summers and savage, slashing winters. It tolerated these hardships. But, the ancient grandmother suffered mightily under the meanness fostered on it as a hanging tree.

Elijah Red Horse found his brother Micah Little Fox hanging from a stout limb late in the afternoon, two days after the noose tightened around his neck, choking off life. Crows plucked out blood-filled eyeballs, leaving empty sockets staring sightless across the grass sea. These and other scavengers gnawed on the man, ravishing his human-ness, leaving only ripped clothes and the medicine bag to identify the earth-red body.

Elijah did not fault the crows or other creatures picking morsels from his brother. They were part of the greater ebb and flow of life around mother earth. The medicine bag held the essence of the dead man.

Nor could Elijah fault the bay mare that bolted away from

some cowboy's quirt, leaving her rider to strangle blue. He could not even fault the hired hand from whose wrist that same quirt might still dangle. The fault lay between Micah and the man that commanded the riders.

Elijah legged his horse toward the dangling corpse. The dun gelding snorted and whirled away from the death scent several times before he could be maneuvered close enough for the hanging rope to be cut. The man carefully lowered his brother back to earth, although there was no longer a need for gentleness.

A half-breed, he honored his Indian blood by wrapping the dead body in a saddle blanket and placing him high in the grandmother's arms. Dry, hot wind whispered a death song. It curled around the grandmother oak with her burden, spilled down the knoll and sank into the rolling waves of grass.

Elijah found a trail of unshod horses herding cattle, accompanied by a wagon with a bent wheel. He saw that, for two days, Micah had ridden point for the wagon and riders. He had helped butcher a cow. The group divided the cattle and splintered into several small groups, moving west and north into Indian Territory. Micah took nothing when he rode alone toward the southeast and Fort Smith.

Sign told a tale of shod horses striking Micah's track and a running struggle ending at the ancient tree. Elijah's white blood curdled and cried for revenge. His Indian blood understood a story of hunger and desperation.

A day slid past before he tracked Micah's bay and shod horses to a corral at Jess Young's River Y Ranch. A lavender dusk had crept across the hard-pack ranch yard by the time he rode within sight of the buildings. Several cow hands lounged around the well, smoking hand-rolled cigarettes. A lantern cast a weak light across the clapboard bunk house porch. Dust powder floated around the men's boots as they shuffled to and fro, ending their evening chores.

Elijah dismounted and waited in the tree shadows. He stroked the neck of his horse, keeping it quiet and still.

When the last of the lights were extinguished and the yard appeared settled for the night, he slowly circled around the far side of the corral leading the horse, careful to minimize their silhouettes against the dying light. He made a cold camp in a scrub-choked dry wash just beyond the ranch yard. There he hobbled the dun on the prairie side, beyond the stunted trees. In the morning he'd have time enough to handle affairs.

Before first light he caught the gelding, saddled quietly, and squatted, watching the ranch yard wake. Pink light pried open the morning, turned orange, and promised another hot day. Cloud mountains were already forming across the east with no hint of rain for the parched land.

As the sun began to climb above the ridge, a chuck wagon loaded with extra gear and supplies moved out with a great clanging of pots and groaning of leather to the summer camp.

Hired hands caught their mounts and threw on heavy saddles. One roan pony crow-hopped across the corral, rebelling against a day of dust and work.

The sun rose to flame red as riders mounted, ambled out and began driving the old cows and bawling calves north across the dry west pasture, away from the outbuildings, toward the high north ridge and richer summer grass.

Elijah waited until they were out of ear-shot before he walked toward the barn corral. The morning air was sodden and already he felt the prickle of rising sweat.

A grizzled foreman, last to ride out, finished cinching up and appeared out of the barn darkness. He looked hard at Elijah, rubbed leather-broken hands down his horse's shoulder, and flicked a quirt against his chaps. Its soft slapping sound belied its cutting sting against living flesh.

"What's a breed like you doing out of the territory?" His voice carried a note of menace. His face, spiderwebbed from harsh years in the sun, gave no quarter.

He did not wait for an answer but mounted and turned his cowpony to face the Indian. "You need to be riding on. Your kind's not wanted around here."

Elijah squinted up at the rider, flicked the reins against his leather leggings, and nodded. "Yep." The two men eyed each other.

"Mind if I water my horse?" He did not wait for a reply but allowed the dun a morning drink from the ranch trough. "I need another horse to take into the territory. You sell me that bay?"

"River Y don't sell to breeds." The voice was hard and steady, the eyes blank, unreadable.

"What about that big grey? He looks like he's got a long stride." Elijah stood next to the rough log corral, leaned slightly on the top rail, and looked over the milling horses. They shuffled, tails swishing against the onslaught of flies.

"I told you. I don't aim to repeat. Can't sell you nothing. You need to move on. Besides, the grey is Mr. Young's personal horse." He backed his cowpony away from the Indian before slapping it with his quirt, causing the chestnut to jump forward into a canter. Dust swirled up as horse and man followed the bawling herd.

Elijah stood a moment and watched the rider disappear over the ridgeline. He took the rawhide lariat off his saddle, left the dun ground tied, stepped into the corral and put a loop around the bay, fashioning it into a rope halter. He led the horse outside the enclosure and swung onto the dun's back in one smooth motion.

The ranch house door burst open, slapping loud against the wooden frame. A heavy-set man emerged, his belly pushing tight against his shirt. He tied down his pistol, settled it loose in the holster and stalked toward Elijah.

The breed sat his horse quietly.

"What the hell you think you doing with that horse?" He spoke with a snarl and his proprietary arrogance oozed around him like yellow fog.

"My brother's horse. She needs to carry him on his spirit journey. I'm taking her to him."

"The devil you say. I took that horse off an Injun cow thief. Caught him red handed."

"Maybe you got the wrong man. Maybe you didn't see true. Maybe the judge in Fort Smith only one can do any hanging." The breed looked down at the rancher. "Taking the horse makes you a thief. Hanging a man outside the law makes you bloody."

"You mangy red scavenger. No one accuses me of anything. I own this ranch and everything around here — cattle, horses, men — everything. Even the law."

"Maybe. Maybe not. Maybe there are laws you don't own."

The horses stamped, restless and snorty at the rising hostility. "Brother's already on his journey. He needs his horse. I have to ride."

He legged the dun into a slow walk toward the dark presence of the man. "I tracked this mare here. Someone at the hanging rode a horse that toes out on the left fore, like that grey does."

"You halfbreed red dog. I'd hang the preacher himself before I'd let him call me a murderer and thief and try to take one of my horses. I sure as hell can hang another Injun. I'll see you dead before I let you ride out."

Elijah's boot came out of the stirrup before the man's gun cleared leather, kicking the pistol, letting it skitter across the yard. Sun glinted briefly off the knife blade as the breed dropped low out the saddle, and slashed through the man's gut, spilling white-blue entrails into the hard-pack ground.

The smell of blood and steaming innards caused both horses to shy and side-step away from the slumped man. He knelt for long minutes in the dirt, vainly holding his belly with both hands.

Elijah settled himself on the dun and wiped the blade clean on his pant leg. Without passion, he watched the dying man struggle to hold in his guts.

The halfbreed kicked his horse into a canter, riding west toward the river, leading the bay. He did not look back.

The great oak's arms formed several cradle notches, one of which held Micah. A buffalo knife, simple quirt, medicine bag and crow feather rested on the still form. Near the grandmother, the bay mare lay with her throat gently cut, already racing across time.

Within a year only bleached bones and hair marked the killing ground. It would be another year before late summer lightning struck the majestic oak, burning it and the grass around for miles, releasing its spirit. Finally, winter threw a white blanket across the blackened earth and the season of rest descended.

In the spring, green shoots pushed against the ground, sending up rich sweetness to spread across the knoll, at first timidly, then with growing strength, covering the death scars.

The End

DUKE PENNELL – EDITOR / PUBLISHER

My earliest memories are of sitting on my Grandmother's lap in the tiny burg of Elkville, Illinois, listening to her tell stories of adventure and derring-do. She introduced me to the wonderful world of words, words used to paint pictures in my mind. Those pictures were even more vivid than reality because, as a small child, I couldn't go out and fight villains except vicariously, through the words of a storyteller. I can still recall the tale of "When Grandpa Shot the Whale." Exciting!

Soon, the spoken stories were replaced by written ones. I found books, and I found my place in the world. I didn't have to wait for someone else to find time to tell me a tale; I could experience new adventures whenever I wanted.

But Life's demands come to us all, and school, growing up, girls, military service, family, and work occupied most of my time. While I never lost the love for the words that took me away from the humdrum "real" world, I didn't have the time to dive back into that lovely pool of stories and just float wherever the tide took me. My dips into the stream were brief, hurried things . . . better than nothing, but not what I yearned for.

Then I discovered the Northwest Arkansas Writers Workshop. A fine group of people who said it was OK – no, better than OK – to lose myself in the words, to become another fish in that vast ocean of ideas and feed on them and grow. From those folks, especially founders and mentors Dusty Richards and Velda Brotherton, I learned the craft of writing, and from there turned to helping other writers polish their tales.

FRONTIER TALES EZINE

The ezine Frontier Tales was born out of frustration. I couldn't find anywhere to send my Western stories and Dusty Richards, who has over 100 published books under his belt, told me there was much uncertainty facing authors because of the changes in the publishing industry. Book stores were going out of business and magazines were almost a thing of the past. The year 2009 was a scary time for writers.

I was just a beginner at this fiction-writing business, but I'm a computer engineer and website design is one of my skills. I decided to create an online magazine devoted to Western short stories, and **www.Frontier Tales.com** was born.

A lot of stories have now seen the light of day and a lot of writers, new authors as well as veterans, have gotten exposure they wouldn't have otherwise found. Several of them have told me that Frontier Tales has made the difference in their writing careers. I'll confess, that makes me proud. From October 2009 to February 2012, over 100 stories from writers who also love words and ideas have been available to anyone who has a few minutes to take a trip back to the Old West, and more are coming out each month.

Frontier Tales has received a wonderful reception and reaches viewers from around the world, with readership almost doubling every year. If you're a writer, greenhorn or old hand, consider sending us your polished western frontier prose.

See submission guidelines at www.FrontierTales.com

PEN-L PUBLISHING

Working on the ezine Frontier Tales put me in touch with the publishing side of the writing business and I learned that many authors were not satisfied with their publishers. All part of the changing landscape of the publishing world, I suppose. But I figured there should be a small press that respects writers and creates a high-quality product and experience for them. My wife contributed her skills in editing and marketing and so Pen-L Publishing was born – for the Love of Writing.

Got a book ready for publishing and don't know where to turn? Give us a look at it. Come to **www.Pen-L.com.** We might be just what you're looking for. We don't cater only to Western writers, though. We welcome most all kinds of fiction and non-fiction, as long as it has a distinctive voice or answers the people's greatest needs and questions.

It's another grand adventure in that place I found so long ago . . . the wonderful world of words. I hope you'll join me there.

Made in the USA
Charleston, SC
09 April 2012